MISSING IN MISKATONIC

A Travis Daniels Investigation

JP BEHRENS

Crystal Lake Publishing
Where Stories Come Alive!

www.crystallakepub.com

Copyright © 2024 by JP Behrens
Join the Crystal Lake community today
on our newsletter and Patreon!
https://linktr.ee/CrystalLakePublishing

Download our latest catalog here:
https://geni.us/CLPCatalog

All Rights Reserved

ISBN: 978-1-964398-12-9

Cover Art:
Joanna Halerz | jo.widomska@gmail.com

Layout:
Jacque Day | jacqueday.com

This is a work of fiction. Names, characters, businesses, places, events and incidents are either the products of the author's imagination or used in a fictitious manner. Any resemblance to actual persons, living or dead, or actual events is purely coincidental.

No part of this publication may be reproduced, stored in a retrieval system, or transmitted in any form or by any means, without the prior permission in writing of the publisher, nor be otherwise circulated in any form of binding or cover than that in which it is published and without a similar condition including this condition being imposed on the subsequent purchaser.

Follow us on Amazon:

WELCOME
TO ANOTHER

CRYSTAL LAKE PUBLISHING
CREATION

Join today at www.crystallakepub.com & www.patreon.com/CLP

PRAISE FOR JP BEHRENS

"Travis Daniels is sure to win the hearts of Phillip Marlowe or Sam Spade fans. Readers whose souls answer the call of Cthulhu or are warmed at the mention of Arkham will be just as pleased." – Caleb Jones, Author of *Red Hill Paradise*

"This book is an awesome, out of this world, read. Behrens just keeps on improving with everything he writes. I can't wait for more from Travis, because I enjoyed every single minute that I spent and I want to hang out some more." – No Remorse Reviews

"Behrens' writing is solid and *Missing in Miskatonic* is no exception. Super entertaining!" – Erica Summers, author of *Rictus Grin*

"I was rubbing my goaty little hooves together in excited anticipation. It unfolds in ways that are so satisfying, and just gets bigger and bigger as we approach the finale." – Happy Goat Horror

"This is detective noir mixed with allllll the Lovecraftian vibes!! Lots of shady characters, but I really liked the private detective MC!" – Date with a Thriller Reviews

For my Dad.
He introduced me to Lovecraft, books, and set me on this path.
Much to his chagrin.
He's cool with it now.

And always,
For Stephanie.
Love you.

Contents

New York City	1
Daniels' Investigation	9
Bolton, Massachusetts	15
The Armitage Memorial Library	23
Miskatonic University	33
The Silver Twilight Lodge	43
St. Mary's Hospital	49
Arkham Sanitarium	55
The Laboratory	65
Where Truth Meets Madness	71
Arkham, Massachusetts	77
Coda	85
The End of a Road	

New York City

"It isn't for sale, sir."

"Not my concern. I'm just here to verify its authenticity."

I hated these kinds of cases. Hunting down antiques is bad enough, but adding the stress of ensuring they are what the owner claims is a headache all its own. The research takes weeks of dry, academic reading at the best of times. And when the piece is steeped in mythology and ghost stories, verification can be tricky, if not damn near impossible.

"What does it matter if it is or isn't authentic?"

Lying isn't something I enjoy doing, either. It leaves a bad taste in my mouth and complicates everything. Probably shouldn't have become a private detective, but being a cop didn't sit well either. I've never been a fan of bureaucracy or chains of command. Give me a case and get out of the way. But protecting my client, no matter how weird, was part of the job, so lying was sometimes necessary.

"I'm compiling a book about strange sea myths: Bermuda Triangle, *The Flying Dutchman*, *The Vigilant*, and *The Alert*."

The man winced at the mention of the last two.

"If that idol is authentic," I continued, "I'd love to take a photo of it for my book." The camera hung from my neck to emphasize my innocent intentions. I'd already confirmed the provenance of the idol, and the man's grimace at the name of those last two ships further verified my suspicions. Getting a picture could grease the wheels of getting paid if Madam Bina doubted my work. I placed my hands on the camera as if he'd already consented.

"No, sorry. It's just an oddity I purchased years ago on a whim. I thought it would give the place a touch of mystery." He grasped the bulbous idol and tucked it into a drawer before I could "accidentally" snap a photo.

"Too bad. Thanks, anyway." Walking out of the bookshop, I cast a sideways glance through the front window and watched the proprietor pace back and forth. He worried at his fingernails like a hunted man. In my Buick Roadster, I revved the engine and glided into New York City traffic.

As I cruised along the streets, the city throbbed around me, always alive and forever in motion. Lights flashed all day and night. Everyone was trying to catch someone's attention while I worked to avoid it. It didn't take long to reach Red Hook. A lot of crazy stories floated in and out of the neighborhood, but that wasn't different than any other New York borough. Crazy bred in this city almost as fast as rats and roaches. And only crazy was willing to run around in broad daylight expecting to be treated as normal.

Everyone had a story about every street in the city. Some went back decades. Some went back days. All of them ended with the common lament, "Well, what do you expect when you live in NYC?" That sense of futility didn't stop people from telling the same stories year after year.

A parking spot in front of Madam Bina's shop stood empty, and I pulled in. The casual flow of pedestrians that marked the city on a near-constant basis didn't exist in this part of town. Only a handful of locals, camped out on their stoops, peppered the area. They watched nothing, counting down the seconds until the next meal or fix.

An old, hand-painted wooden sign swung above the doorway of the shop. A jagged crack down the center resembled a child's drawing of a lightning bolt and threatened to split the sign once and for all. Keziah's Curiosities stood between two run-down tenements. Somehow, it had avoided the notice of developers scavenging the depressed city for cheap properties to reimagine into high-rises no one could afford.

Inside the dusty shop, everything was in the exact spot it had always occupied. I braved the clutter of esoteric artifacts, searching for the old woman who owned the place. "Madam Bina?" The aisles formed an endless maze of junk. I hated searching for the old woman every time I came here. The path to her back office always seemed to change in small, annoying ways. She was a good client, however, so I managed.

"Right here, Travis."

I whirled around to find Madam Bina right behind me, as usual. The old woman could be quiet when she wanted.

"I found the idol. The owner of Pickman's Pages has it. Not for sale, he says. Tried to get a photo, but he tucked it into a drawer before I got a chance."

Her eyes glittered above her long, crooked nose. "Oh, what a pity. Well, I only asked you to find it for me. You've done your job, so I guess I should pay you."

"That would be great, Madam Bina."

"Always so polite. That's why I like you, Travis."

"Glad to hear it."

She paused and turned just enough to peer over her shoulder at me. "As well you should be," she said in her raspy, croaking voice. A high-pitched titter followed the odd statement as she continued down the aisles toward the back office. As we passed through the store, I heard skittering behind the cabinets and shelves that clogged the room to the point of bursting.

"I think you have rats."

"Who doesn't around here?"

I couldn't argue with that, though it always surprised me how unflappable Madam Bina could be.

The office was stuffed with more oddities than the main store, if that was possible. Bina rifled around her desk, searching for her money. I noticed a small pile of bloody bandages in the waste can. "You hurt yourself?"

She looked confused until I pointed down.

"Oh! That?" A wide smile stretched across her lips. "Just feeding the rats." She returned to searching through her piles of old manuscripts, totems, dolls, and bones while laughing at her joke. I could only shake my head. The woman was a sweet old lady one second and very unsettling the next. She cackled with delight when she produced an envelope with my name scrawled on it. She handed it over. The thickness felt right. She was weird, but paid well.

Trusting enough to forgo counting it—she always paid what she owed—the envelope went into the inside pocket of my jacket. "You have a good day, Madam Bina."

As always, she guided me toward the front of the store, pointing out the newest acquisitions along the way. She gave my arm a friendly squeeze as I stepped outside. Once the door snapped shut, I hopped into my car and headed back to the office to tie up the paperwork. No matter the job, every one required slogging through paperwork.

My office consisted of a rented room in a squat building near Five Points. I maintained a parking spot in a secure garage nearby. The rent on the garage was higher than the office. Thing was, that the office didn't have anything worth stealing most days. That fact never stopped a few desperate souls from checking, only to leave empty-handed. Despite the shouts and gunfire popping in the distance, the five-block walk down Canal to Mulberry helped clear my mind after every job. Even so, my hand shifted to the S&W Model 10 revolver in my shoulder holster, ready for anyone stupid enough to jump out of the shadows.

When I reached the block my building was on, I searched the area. The normal drunks and homeless haunted the streets. Once I was up the concrete steps to the building's entrance, I released my gun and fished out the key to the front door. Just as it touched the lock, the door swung open, and two block-faced thugs stepped out, flanking me before I could react. I dropped my hand to the side, the key still clenched in my fist.

"How you doin', Daniels?" asked Frances Rossi, the street tough on my left.

"Fine, Tweedle-dee. Have you figured out why a raven is like a writing desk, yet?"

Rossi, who I would never call Frances, squinted at me, unsure if I was mocking him. "Noticed the poor security in your building. Thought we'd stand here and protect the place 'til you got back."

"Thanks. I'll let the super know. That all?"

Rossi stepped closer. Hot breath warmed my face. "You know why we're here, Daniels. Don't mess around."

"Can't get blood from a rock."

"You'd be surprised, Daniels."

The silent thug on my right, Anton Brambilla, reached into my jacket and withdrew the envelope like he could smell it. "My apologies, Anton. *You* must be Tweedle-dee."

Frances snapped out a quick punch to my gut. I tensed my abs, knowing it was coming, but those hits still hurt. Apparently, he understood some of my children's fiction insults. "Keep it up, Daniels. Mr. Castaigne may like your wise-ass comments, but I don't." He glanced at Anton. "He got enough there?"

Anton shook his head as he tucked the envelope into his inner pocket.

"The boss is gonna need some collateral until you pay the rest, Daniels. Too bad that car of yours isn't here. Long walk back to the house." Frances reached into my jacket. "I always did like that piece of yours, though."

In a flash, I jammed the key into his throat, forcing Frances to his toes, and snapped a kick into Anton's inner thigh. A little lower and the bones and cartilage would have been destroyed, but I liked and respected Anton. He tumbled down the steps as I pushed the key a little deeper into Frances' throat. "Keep it up, Tweedle-dum."

"Agostino will kill you."

"I doubt it. Like you said, he likes me."

"I'm his nephew!"

"Still, he likes me more."

I shoved Frances down the steps into Anton's arms. With my revolver in hand, I unlocked the door. "Agostino'll get his money, but no one touches my car or my gun. No one."

Frances glared, twitching to reach for his own gun. Anton placed a heavy hand on Frances' shoulder and urged him to walk away. Anton offered me a half-smile and nod while brushing the dirt from his suit. When they had disappeared around the corner about a block away, I headed upstairs.

The filthy yellow walls glowed under flickering lights. They hung from the ceiling by single wires, illuminating the chips of paint that lay scattered across the rough, wooden floorboards. The door to my office was open a crack, the frame busted at the lock. I stepped in and sighed.

Everything was in shambles. They'd not only broken in but searched the place like a pack of rabid Neanderthals. Was it too much to ask for a little mutual professionalism? Anton knew how not to make a mess of it while still letting the target know he'd been there.

Goddamned Frances...

Daniels' Investigation

Life as a private detective was never simple, especially in 1928 with Prohibition. Deal with enough philandering spouses, stolen "family heirlooms," and mob turf wars, you develop flint skin and eyes on the back and sides of your head. I flipped the file closed on the tracked idol. Madam Bina was a kook, but I had bills to pay. The jobs she offered were always simple, if not easy. Track this or that down, make sure it's real, see if they'll sell. More often than not, they ended up selling or trading to Bina. Either way, I got paid.

I slipped the file into my cabinet alongside the others concerning artifacts Bina wanted me to find. The bottle of malt whiskey I removed from the same cabinet was to celebrate another successful day ending with "Y." Shocking how often that happened.

I found a clean glass in my top right drawer and poured out a triple. Only savages and alcoholics drink something this good straight from the bottle. The bottle disappeared back into the cabinet to prevent me from drinking more. Who knew when I'd come across another good bottle again? I sipped while listening to the traffic outside. A cacophony of engines, brakes, and angry voices rattled the thin glass windows. I took another sip and considered the mess strewn across my office. Where to start?

Before a decision could be made, a *tap, thump, thump* approached. The steady rhythm remained at the same volume the entire time, like someone was standing outside my office door, tapping out the same metronome-esque beat. Still, I knew whoever was walking along the hallway was getting closer. I eased back into my chair to look casual and wrapped my hand around the sawed-off shotgun mounted on a swivel under my desk. After running into Frances and Anton, this wasn't a time to take chances.

A shadow stepped into view behind the frosted glass of my door. Three heavy, sharp knocks shook the flimsy wooden frame.

Without waiting for a response, invitation, or warning, the door creaked open. A skeletal old man strode into the room dressed in a suit made of the blackest fabric I'd ever seen. It shimmered a dim purple as he moved and fit his slim frame as if tailored for him by the greatest, most exclusive tailor in existence. Tiny pinpricks of light flickered in and out of the fabric like stars being born and dying at the same time. He surveyed the room with deep-set, gleaming eyes.

"Can I help you?" I asked.

The man focused on me and scoffed. He stepped forward to take the seat opposite me and removed the top hat I was only now noticing. He set it atop his cane. I glimpsed the multifaceted gemstone affixed to the top of the cane for only a second before the hat hid it from view. Even with that short exposure, an otherworldly palette of colors swarmed my mind, threatening to unbalance me to the depths of my soul. The old man coughed, and my attention snapped back to those hungry eyes and the almost translucent skin. I could see blue veins pulsing within.

"My name is Sir Edward Martin Mandeville. My associates name you as a man of some worth. I wish to hire you."

I remained silent. Everything about this guy creeped me out.

He grinned as if aware of my aversion and reveled in it. "My niece has gone missing from her home in Bolton, Massachusetts."

He settled back into the chair, awaiting my response. Most of the time, I could give a client a thousand-yard stare that would provoke nervous talk and let slip additional, unintended information about a case. It helped me avoid problematic cases. This guy appeared ready to wait out doomsday and then some.

"Listen, Mister—"

"Sir."

"Ok, *Sir* Mandeville. I don't normally take jobs outside the city, let alone that far north. Who'd you say recommended me?"

"I didn't."

"I'm sorry—"

"I understand your reluctance, Mr. Daniels. Of course, I will pay you well for the inconvenience."

"I'm not sure you understand—"

Mandeville withdrew a thick envelope. I had no idea where it came from. Something that thick should have bulged in his suit, but the jacket remained sculpted to the man's chest before and after the reveal of the *very* thick envelope. Most of the time, I'd clock a stack of bills or gun hiding under someone's jacket. It was like Mandeville conjured the envelope from nothing with those long, spindly fingers. I blinked several times, trying to make sense of those fingers. Too many joints articulated each too-long digit. The envelope slapped down onto the table, and my attention was stolen by the pile of twenties spilling out. There had to be over $7,000 there.

I tore my scowl away from the money and said, "No."

"Pardon me?"

"No way. No one pays that kind of money to find a girl. Find someone else."

Mandeville leered. It wasn't a grin. It was a leer. The sight took my breath away. Rows of tightly packed needle teeth glinted under the dim lights of my office. A sudden burning forced my eyes closed. I rubbed at them to clear away the pain. When I reopened my eyes, the wide smile remained. His teeth were normal and nicotine-stained, creating the illusion of nightmarish needles.

"Are you ok, Mr. Daniels?"

"Yeah, fine. Just tired and overworked."

"Yes, I hear you are very good at what you do, Mr. Daniels. I would not have come if I wasn't absolutely sure you were the right man for this job."

The pile of money glowed on my desk, teasing and tempting me.

"The girl means a lot to you?"

"Oh, you misunderstand. I care nothing for the child. Her parents are distant family members, and when the girl went missing, they contacted me. I am only facilitating this to quiet them. Since the disappearance, they have bothered me endlessly. I wish for this matter to be cleared up so I may return to my solitude and studies."

"You're a professor or something?"

"Or something, yes."

"A kind of scholar? You working on a book?"

Mandeville's eye glinted. "As you say."

One last look at the damnable pile of money forced the next question out of my mouth. "What's the kid's name?"

"Leslie Owens. Disappeared more than a week ago."

"You got a picture?"

"No, but I can provide the parents' address. I'm sure they can provide all that you need."

We stared at each other in silence. For the first time since Mandeville entered my office, I noticed all the background noise of the city had faded away. Part of me wanted to look out the window, to find reassurance in the world outside. Another, larger part of me refused to turn my back on Mandeville. Buried under those two aspects of my psyche, a squirming fear whispered a warning of what I might see if I was foolish enough to pull back the curtains.

"Do we have a deal, Mr. Daniels?" Mandeville reached out his bony hand with its polished nails and bulbous knuckles.

The money sat in the middle of my desk, promising to wipe out numerous debts. I reached out and took Mandeville's hand, cursing myself as I did, both figuratively and literally. Mandeville's thin claws wrapped around my hand. It felt like an electrified vise had clamped down and sent a jolt through my entire body. Mandeville kept smiling while I remained paralyzed. Flashes of white lights burst in my eyes and were replaced by dancing black spots. When he released the connection, I fell into my seat and heard his voice drive screws into my brain.

"You'll find the girl's parents in Bolton, Massachusetts." With a flourish of his unnatural fingers, he produced a card with the address written on the back and snapped it down with ear-popping finality. "Good evening, Mr. Daniels."

Mandeville stood up, bowed, and left the office. The same *tap, thump, thump* resonated back down the hall. When it stopped, all the horns, engines, and yells from the street below flooded back in a wave. I stared down at the pile of money before sliding open the cabinet drawer, removing the whiskey, and taking a gulp straight from the bottle.

Bolton, Massachusetts

The duffel bag stuffed with my clothes, gun, and ammo hit the passenger seat with a dull, but solid, thump. I hated the idea of traveling hours north, but the money gave me a way to pay my debts and maybe relax a little before the next financial crisis ambushed me.

The drive was the definition of bucolic: clean air, open fields, and colorful trees. Even on major highways there were so many trees you'd think New England was connected by nothing but backroads. I drove through what passed for a major city in Connecticut and chuckled at the small, squat buildings and open sky. Massachusetts wasn't much better until I hit Boston. Bigger than Hartford and New Haven, Boston was still a baby compared to New York. There was something charismatic about the stunted skyline that made one consider retiring there someday. That daydream faded when the car hit the tangle of winding roads that wrapped around and through local mountains. Retirement wasn't something I had a chance of with all the debt hanging over my head.

My route took me north past Salem. I'd done some basic research, which was complicated by the oddity that there were in fact two towns named Bolton in Massachusetts. Lucky for me, only one had the address Mandeville had provided for the Owens. There had been some kind of natural disaster in the town decades ago. Long stretches of land were razed to the ground to save the remaining unaffected areas, but the town had never really recovered. Perhaps that was how a second Bolton was able to exist. Was it a way to brush the tragedy under the rug?

Vast fields lay barren along stretches of country roads that led into the small farming community. The old shacks seemed to teeter when the wind blew. Gray, worn-down residents stared with sunken eyes as my car rumbled by. Maybe Mandeville's sunken appearance was a family trait. Even the children appeared listless, ignoring the bright new car rolling past. Most jumped too close after my Roadster.

Farther along the downtown area, if it could be called that, stood a large tombstone-like building amidst a handful of empty, dilapidated shacks. While the shacks appeared long abandoned and in desperate need of repair or condemnation, the larger building maintained a semblance of continued maintenance. A faded wooden sign nailed across the face of the building stated "SUNDRY GOODS" in large block letters. I pulled up and got out. The loamy aroma of fertilizer slapped me in the face. As I coughed on my way into the store, a group of sour old men who had been concentrating on a checkerboard glared at me. A glance at the board showed that black had the game sewn up.

Inside, shelves lined the room. They were filled with flour and rice, drab fabric and spools of yarn, sleeves of paper and packs of pencils, and paperback books and maps. I picked up a local map and approached the counter. It appeared to double as a butcher's block and checkout register.

The cashier chewed on his tobacco while glancing from the map to me. He tapped the button without looking away or blinking. I dropped a nickel on the counter and nodded. The old men returned to staring at their checkerboard. Nothing had changed from what I could see. They remained fixated on the pieces. Neither man moved to finish the game or talk.

Back in the car, I thought, "The sooner I'm back in the city, the better." With the map unfolded over the duffel, I found a path leading to the Owens' house.

They didn't live too far outside of the crumbling downtown area. Their fields lay choked with weeds and the barn leaned to the left, open and empty. Its door swung idly in the wind, squeaking in a semi-steady rhythm. My knock on their door echoed like thunder through an empty home. While reaching for Mandeville's card to double-check I had the right address, it flung open. A haggard couple with dark, sleepless eyes stared through me.

"Sir, ma'am, I'm Travis Daniels. Sir Mandeville hired me to find your daughter. Do you have some time to discuss the matter?"

Wide-eyed and unfocused, they shuffled away from the door to allow me in. Cracked plaster walls stretched down the hall into a cold, dark kitchen. The sitting area to the left had a beaten, dusty easy chair and a moth-ravaged sofa. I motioned to the chair. "May I?"

The couple lurched to the sofa and took their seats without speaking. A cloud of dust bloomed around them. They didn't seem to notice. I eased down into the chair, hoping to limit the amount of dust I disturbed. The smell of rot and stale air hung stagnant. The walls were bare. Faint outlines stained the walls where pictures once hung, ghosts of an erased past. Light streamed in from the curtainless windows, illuminating the room well enough. A thin film of grime and scuff marks marred the hardwood floor.

"I know this is difficult, but what can you tell me about Leslie?"

The girl's name sent a spark of life through her parents, stirring them from their stupor. "Oh, she was the kindest soul you ever knew," the mother said.

"Was? Do you think she's dead?"

Mr. Owens shouted, "No!" Then he lowered his voice. "I mean, no. It's just been so hard these last few days. No sleep. We can't eat. We can't leave." He stared around the room as if terrified by the bland, empty walls. "We can't leave."

"I understand," I said. "I'll do my best to find her. Where was the last place she was seen?"

"The Armitage Memorial Library at Miskatonic University. She's a student there studying..." Mr. Owens paused, working the unfamiliar words through his lips. "Anthropological Folklore."

"We knew something was wrong when she didn't come home during the school break," Mrs. Owens said. "She would never miss a chance to come home."

I glanced around the room again, figuring I'd find the girl still at school. I wouldn't blame her for not coming back. "Do you have a picture of her?"

Mrs. Owens jumped up, rushed over to a side table, and pulled a picture out of the drawer. This was the first bit of real energy I'd seen from either of them. She moved with a kind of desperation to get the picture into my hands.

The girl in the picture stared into the camera, smiling. Dark hair, bright eyes, button nose, and full lips; she was the kind of girl who could get caught up in all kinds of unsavory situations. I put the picture in my inner pocket and stood. "Can I see her room, by chance?"

Both parents looked at each other. Mr. Owens asked, "Why?"

"Just to get a feeling for the kind of person she is." *And to know why you don't want me to.* "It can be helpful."

He stood up, straining to move, and motioned for the stairs. "Not much up there. She took everything to college with her." I nodded my understanding.

The steps creaked under our weight. Some sagged, threatening to give. The upstairs smelled dank and musty. Most of the doors were closed. Shadows filled the thin hallway. Mr. Owens stepped with care, always watching his footing. He examined each door before moving on, as if lost in his own house. At the second door to the left, he stopped, stared at it, held his breath, and pointed.

"This one."

I smiled and joked, "You sure?"

He never took his eyes off the door, as if it might attack or disappear if he did. He didn't laugh, either. He stood there, pointing.

The door whined open on rusty hinges. The room appeared naked, consisting of a stained mattress on the floor, cobwebs covering the walls, and bits of plaster strewn across the floor like rubble. The closet door hung from busted hinges, ready to break free and clatter to the floor. The cracked glass in the windows was coated with green mildew.

"You weren't kidding when you said she took everything."

"We can't sleep. Can't eat." He stared at me with harrowed, pleading eyes. Tears shimmered there, on the edge of tumbling over.

"I'll find her."

The room wasn't going to tell me anything, so I retreated down the stairs. Mrs. Owens stood at the base of the steps, waiting, staring past me. A worried anticipation gripped her until Mr. Owens clamored down behind me. His footsteps were rushed and impatient.

"Well, thank you for the picture. I've never heard of Miskatonic. Where is that located?"

Mrs. Owens' eyes widened, as if I'd asked the most idiotic question ever uttered.

"You'll find it in Arkham. South of here."

"I've heard of Arkham, saw some signs on my way up here. It had some trouble with the FBI a few years back, didn't it?"

"I wouldn't know anything about that," Mr. Owens said in a rush, casting the subject to the wind.

"I won't trouble you any further."

"Good luck, Mr. Daniels," Mrs. Owens said with a light touch on my elbow.

I smiled and let myself out of the house. Behind me, I heard the familiar sound of frustration and sobbing. The dry earth crackled under my feet as I walked. The map I had purchased showed Arkham just south of Bolton. Once there, I was sure I could get directions to the school with little effort. Making a repeat visit to Bolton's Sundry Goods held no temptation.

Through a cloud of dirt kicked up by my wheels, I gave the house one last glance. Both Mr. and Mrs. Owens stood in the doorway, staring out. Mr. Owens held his hand up as if waving goodbye, but he wasn't moving and looked flat from a distance, as if pushed up against glass. Mrs. Owens held her hands to her mouth, eyes wide with terror. With no children of my own, I didn't know the pain and worry they must be going through.

Driving down the road toward Arkham, I hoped to discover good news and ease their suffering. A casual glance out of my rearview mirror showed the house shrinking into the distance. The Owenses stood at the door, crying into each other's arms as the door closed.

The Armitage Memorial Library

The town of Arkham rivaled Boston in age, but little else. Few men and women bustled along the streets. None of the buildings stood more than three stories high. It looked more like a great, sprawling village that had chosen to grow out rather than up. The buildings were packed tight against each other, eliminating alleys. Every structure leaned a few inches over the street as if designed to blot out the sun. Not a single one looked to have been built any later than 1890. A city frozen in time, unwilling or incapable of moving forward.

Driving around, trying to understand the strange town, I passed a building of flat, grey slate with windows dotting its face. The Derleth Hotel was the first location I'd seen since entering Arkham that wasn't some small, ramshackle boarding house. After securing a parking spot up the road, I grabbed my bag and headed for the hotel, hoping for a room. The lobby was little more than ugly carpeting connected to worse wallpaper. A wooden desk at the base of two curving steps leading to a second floor was attended by an ancient-looking man. There were two hallways stretching out behind the stairs. I suspected I would find the same mirrored above.

"You have any rooms?"

The attendant pointed to a wall full of room keys. I swore I saw dust fall from his stiff uniform and heard his creaking joints.

"One bed, attached bathroom, if you have it."

He shuffled over to the wall and ran a finger over the keys, creating a series of clicks and tings until he found the key he wanted and pulled it down. "Five dollars a night," the attendant said with the graveled voice of a heavy smoker. The key clattered onto the desk to punctuate the cost.

I handed over a twenty, hoping I wouldn't need to be in town that long. The tab on the key stated 217, and it was about halfway down the hallway on the second floor. More ugly carpeting and wallpaper greeted me when I entered the room. Tossing my bag on the bed, I used the bathroom to freshen up after the long day of driving. I retrieved my gun and some ammo from the bag. With the gun loaded and holstered, it was time to check out the college.

Back at the front desk, I asked, "You got any maps of the town?"

The attendant reached out a palsied hand, pointing behind me. A small stand, almost empty and covered in shadows and cobwebs, hid in the corner. There were faded flyers for events and museums and some menus. The only pile of clean paper was the stack of maps arranged down the middle in a neat line. I took one in hand, waved, and set out. The map showed the college wasn't too far, so I decided to walk and get a feel for Arkham. No one lingered nearby, eyeing my car with nefarious interest, so I felt secure in keeping it where it was.

As I strolled along the red brick sidewalks, weeds poking out from the cracks between the bricks, Arkham loomed dark and ominous. Perhaps it was the quiet way people rushed along the streets, contrary to the uproarious din of New York, that bothered me. Or it may have been how the subtle slant of the buildings blocked the light and the unsettling fog fell over everything, giving the streets an aura of mysterious threat.

A building made up of splintered wood and impossible angles towered over a wide intersection, arching and stretching like a plant determined to follow the sun. Along the walk, I felt the urge to pause under the few beams of unfiltered sunlight that cut through the ever-present gloom. None of them lasted long before a cloud glided across to steal away the light and heat.

As Miskatonic University appeared in the distance, I hoped for a sun-dappled campus full of happy students and befuddled professors. Closer, I found cold stone buildings, austere and solemn, like great mausoleums dedicated to the commemoration and preservation of hoarded knowledge. The campus felt more like a haunted monastery than a place dedicated to the higher purpose of teaching and learning. Serious-looking young men and women hurried from building to building, huddled together, hugging books and supplies close to their chests.

None of the students paid me any attention when I tried to wave one closer, hoping to get directions to the library. I eventually found a large, faded sign displaying a map of the university. The library appeared to be deep in the center of the campus down a circuitous path. The student body continued to ignore my attempts to talk with any of them. It was odd how all of them took great care to remain on the brick paths and avoid cutting across the grounds. The lawn, though tinted yellow, appeared well-tended, but when did college students forgo the fastest route to their classes to avoid trampling on some grass?

The pathway to the library connected to a large fountain set in the center of an open area outlined by a circle of massive constructs made from boulders. Paths branched out from the fountain in various directions, some passing under the thresholds created by the stone constructs, while others swirled around forming random, nonsensical triangles and circles. On the fountain stood the bronze statue of a man reading from an open book with a childish drawing of a branch barren of leaves etched into the cover.

Off to the right, I spotted my destination, an ornate building with great columns climbing up to a vaulted dome over the entrance. Above the doors, the words "The Armitage Memorial Library" were chiseled into the bone-white marble edifice. Two wooden doors mounted in a heavy metal frame towered in front of me. The metal handles affixed to the doors were warm to the touch in defiance of the cold New England weather. Both doors swung open on silent, well-oiled hinges.

Inside, a larger domed ceiling showed a massive mosaic depicting some kind of battle between enormous nightmare gods and barrel-shaped, star-headed creatures with wings. Tearing my attention away from the disturbing scene, I scanned the empty second-floor balcony and headed for the main desk. A young man sent a confused glance my way before closing the book he'd been going through. He stood and came around to the front of the desk to meet me.

"Can I help you?"

"Hopefully," I said, closing the distance and trying to ignore the sensation of having entered a private museum rather than a university library. "I'm trying to track down a student whose family believes she's gone missing. Her name is Leslie Owens."

The boy shrugged. "Doesn't ring a bell, but we get a lot of students in and out."

A glance around showed that to be a lie. I flashed the picture in front of him. An involuntary smile flickered over his lips. "You remember her now, though?" My own smile in response to his obvious crush.

"Yeah, she's a hard one to miss, I guess." He shrugged, embarrassed by his inadvertent admission.

Though known as a place of quiet, the library held none of the ambient sounds one might expect. It was like a tomb with books. "Could I get a look at her library card, maybe? What was she working on?"

"Well, I'm not..."

A couple of bills materialized in my hand and silenced the kid. He stepped behind the desk to a long filing cabinet. "Owens, you said?" As if he didn't know her name.

"Yeah, Leslie Owens." Funny what the promise of a few extra dollars can do.

The kid found the card and pulled it out. There was a long list of books recorded along its length. "Looks like she was doing research in the Rare Books section."

"You know which books?"

"No. This desk only records people going in there. There's a record of requests back there, however, if she ever asked for assistance."

I added a few more bills to his pocket and off we went through the cold, lonely library. Every book was bound in dark, aged leather. I didn't see any of the popular pulp novels, colorful book spines, or classic literature I could pick up at The Strand on Fourth. It was reminiscent of Pickman's Pages with the same aura of sterility. "This whole place looks like a rare books section."

"Yeah, Dr. Armitage, the previous head librarian, felt that this library should only curate books useful to scholars and serious students. Arkham has a town library for more 'frivolous pursuits.' His words."

"What makes the Rare Books section so special?"

"No idea. Dr. Armitage set it up and personally curated those books. He also mandated several of the restrictions we have for the section before his passing. Dr. Llanfer oversees it now, though not as closely as Dr. Armitage was said to."

At the back of the library, we came to a wooden door painted black and etched with silver. A small plaque named the area as the Rare Books section. Anyone not searching for it would pass it by without notice. The door gave off a kind of purple sheen under the limited light. The kid fished out a set of keys from his pocket, unlocked the door, and entered. The room was lined with lanterns and mirrors set to reflect the light to maximum effect. I got the impression that whoever set up the lighting system was determined to never be caught in the dark or near a shadow while working with books.

The kid slipped behind a small desk and set to rifling through the files, searching for the catalog of requested books. He pulled it out and scanned the entries.

"You want a list of titles, or you want to see the books?"

"Are they available?"

"Of course. No one is allowed to remove any of the volumes from this room for any reason."

"What about in case of a fire?" I chuckled until I saw the shadow pass over the kid's face.

"Not even then. That's how…" He shook off whatever he was going to say. "Never mind. You want to see those books?"

"Yeah, sure." After the kid disappeared into the stacks, I wondered what he was about to say, but couldn't think of a good reason to pursue that line of questioning. I doubt an old fire had any bearing on my current case and would only muddy the investigation. When the kid returned, he carried a pile of dusty, fragile tomes in his arms. He placed them on a nearby table.

"Be careful, please. Some of these books are one-of-a-kind, I'm told."

He disappeared into the stacks again to search for more of the volumes Leslie had been researching. As a rough, forceful guy, due to my job, I was never comfortable in museums. I always put my meaty hands into my pockets to prevent touching anything, scared I'd break history itself. Now, in the presence of one-of-a-kind books, I was terrified. I took a seat and read over the titles I could understand. Leslie had been researching books like The *Necronomicon, The Pnakotic Manuscripts, Cryptomenyisis Patefacta, The King in Yellow, The Parchments of Pnom,* and the

Unaussprechlichen Kulten. I was able to flip through some of the pages of the *Necronomicon* before the kid brought back another pile of books, most of which were written in a language foreign and unreadable. Even without being able to read the additional titles or cross-check the list in front of me, I examined the pictures and diagrams illustrated in most of the books. It appeared Leslie had dedicated a great deal of time to investigating many old and dark traditions.

"I've never seen anything like this," I whispered to myself, running a hand over the cover of one of the thicker tomes. The leather felt odd. It was different than the old books I'd been hired to track down in the past for Madam Bina and other wealthy clients.

"No doubt," the kid replied with pride. "Miskatonic University maintains the largest collection of arcane writings and occult knowledge in the U.S. Possibly the largest in the world. Take that book, for instance. One of only two suspected remaining original copies of the *Necronomicon*. The other is supposedly hidden away in the Middle East."

Old habits forced the question from my mouth. "What makes you sure it's authentic?" I drew closer, determined to know why the cover felt so peculiar.

"Oh, that's easy. The binding is human skin."

My hand froze. I pulled away and took several deep breaths. I had heard of the practice but never encountered it during my searches for antiquities. "Remarkable." I choked the word out past my rising revulsion.

"If you flip it over, I swear you can see a spot where the binder used part of a face and stitched an eyelid closed."

I forced a smile and waved off his enthusiasm. "Thanks, but no. I'll take your word for it."

He shrugged. "Are you ok? Need anything else?"

"Actually, yeah. You wouldn't know who her advisor might have been?"

"Depends on her major."

I withdrew a notepad and flipped through it. "Anthropological Folklore?"

"That makes sense, considering the books. Give me a few minutes. I'll look into it for you."

After the kid left, I glanced over the books, reluctant to touch any of the leather-bound ones. I used the eraser of a pencil to lift more covers and peek at the paper and writing. Most of the texts appeared handwritten, produced well before the invention of the printing press. One book stood out as a recent printing. *The King in Yellow* was a modern paperback with a black cover and yellow lettering with a yellow hooded figure staring out. I pulled the book closer. There were no markings on it naming a publisher or author, only the black cover and yellow art. I flipped the book open to a random page.

"Sorry about the delay, mister! Took me a while to track down a name for you."

The sudden statement caused me to flinch. The book slapped closed as it fell to the table.

"Delay? You just left."

"What? I've been gone for twenty minutes. You get caught up in reading? This stuff is spooky, but interesting." The kid held out a slip of paper, smiling at me.

"I guess." I took the paper and read the name. "Professor Harold Whitmore?"

"Yeah, he's the head of the AnthroLore department. I couldn't track down her specific advisor. No one seemed to be able to remember, but he said to come talk to him and he'd help in any way he could."

"Great, thanks." I closed my eyes. A sudden burning stung me all the way to my brain. Flashes of yellow fabric and a black, rotting hand appeared behind my eyelids, then faded.

"You, ok?"

"Yeah, been a long day. Just tired." I pulled out another ten and handed it to the kid. "Thanks for the help."

He smiled at the bill and said, "You bet, mister. Hope you find the girl."

Me too, I thought.

Miskatonic University

By taking an updated map of the Miskatonic campus from the library lobby, I managed to find my way around much faster. The path to the Sciences Building brought me by more oblong boulders, except these appeared to have sprouted from the ground. A few feet away from the stones was an old stone table, or maybe an altar, that had been cordoned off. On top, there appeared to be brown stains and mold growing that glittered with a peculiar shade of purple in the daylight. A college prank gone wrong?

No matter where I roamed, I found few students or teachers. At normal colleges, after any long break, campuses bustle with activity as everyone struggles to fall back into their class schedules. Everything about this school felt wrong. The sooner I could leave, the better.

The front hall of the Sciences Building was illuminated by feeble light dribbling through windows that lined the first floor. A sign pointed the way to the Anthropology Department. Echoes of my footsteps drummed through the empty hallways. As I approached a corner, a sudden nausea overtook me. I leaned against the beige-painted cinder block wall to keep from collapsing. The urge to run washed over my body like a fever.

Before I could move again, a six-foot-tall, pitch-black figure of a man rounded the corner. He strode past, flashing a luminous white smile. His skin and clothes absorbed all the light, creating a kind of moving, inky void. Every feature, curve, wrinkle, and layer was still perceptible while simultaneously blending into the solid, walking shadow. The nausea blossomed in my belly, crawled up, and squeezed my lungs. My vision blurred and went spotty as flashing colors and blots of black danced between me and the world.

Then, everything stopped.

My vision cleared. My lungs began functioning like normal. The nausea and terrible panic that had been dragging me down evaporated, and the hallway was empty. Whoever the shadow-man was, he'd gone. Maybe it was the way the shadows hit him at just the right moment, but at the time I'd been sure that what passed me wasn't human. After a few deep breaths, I concluded I was overtired, seeing things, and just needed some real rest. But first, the interview with Leslie's department head.

I shook off the episode and turned the corner. The Anthropological Folklore Department was two doors down on the left. A young receptionist greeted me as I entered. "Can I help you, sir?"

"Looking for a Professor Harold Whitmore."

"Do you have an appointment?"

"After a fashion."

"May I ask what this is regarding?"

"It's a private affair."

"Ok!" A flash of intrigue stirred her into action. "One moment."

She left her desk and disappeared around a row of towering file cabinets and papers. The room was clogged with cluttered desks, piles of old books and papers, more file cabinets, and strange, dusty artifacts the professors seemed willing to lay anywhere in the open.

"Sir?" the receptionist called. "This way."

Whitmore's office was at the end of a thin, cramped corridor lined with more books, artifacts, papers, and file cabinets. The receptionist glided down the hall with the assurance of practice. She stepped into an empty nook and smiled as I passed. The door stood open, and a man dressed in an ill-fitting suit wavered between sitting and standing, awkward in the throes of etiquette indecision. With a full head of salt-and-pepper hair and black-rimmed glasses, he didn't look the part of the absent-minded educator or the dashing inspirer of generations of students. The receptionist closed the door as she left. The sound of her footsteps, muffled or otherwise, was absent. My smile at the professor as we shook hands was two-fold. If schmoozing the professor didn't work, a secretary with a penchant for eavesdropping would serve as a viable alternative.

"What can I do for you, sir?" Whitman took his seat, running his hands over his papers in a mimicry of rearranging a chaotic desk. A small collection of stones or bones fell into an open drawer. "Ms. Helms said it was a private matter?"

"I've been hired by the family of Leslie Owens to determine her current whereabouts."

A look of fear flashed over Whitmore's face before he feigned confusion and concern. "That is deeply troubling. She's a good student and a talented researcher."

It was interesting that he hadn't expected my coming or knew of the matter. Had the kid at the library known more than he was willing to say but led me to where I needed to be?

"Who is her academic advisor? I'd like to know what she was working on before she disappeared."

"As a matter of fact, I'm her advisor." He leaned back in his chair. "As for what she was researching, nothing too uncommon for her major: witchcraft, demon worship, cults, occult-related insanity. Nothing abnormal."

"Nothing abnormal?"

Whitmore chuckled. "Not here, no. Arkham has a storied history full of strange folktales and rumors. Our school boasts one of the greatest collections of esoteric and occult writings."

"I've seen. The library records show Leslie's research to be leaning a bit beyond local wives' tales."

"You've been to our library already?" His voice raised an octave as he asked the question, as if delighted I'd discovered their wonderful treasure. After years of interviews with talented liars and conmen, the professor couldn't hide the worry in his voice.

"I have. I spent some time in the Rare Books section. Interesting reading in there. I didn't notice much on local customs, though."

Whitmore shifted in his chair, glancing around the room. His eyes flickered to the door. The only door. The one I was sitting in front of. "Well, that's not entirely accurate. Many of the legends talk about how past residents of Arkham are entangled with many of those texts. Did you happen to peruse any of the *Necronomicon*?"

"I saw it." My skin crawled with the memory of how it felt.

"That volume alone contains references to gods and cults that persist in today's society."

"Would any of those groups exist locally?"

Whitmore stood up to withdraw a handkerchief from his pocket and began cleaning the lenses of his glasses, avoiding my eyeline. His forced laughter carried the fear of a man cornered. "Oh, I doubt that. After the raids on Innsmouth a few years back and the indecent in Dunwich before that, most of the undesirables scattered or were run out of town."

"Did Leslie give any indication she was heading anywhere to do further research?" I was curious if he'd jump on the chance to send me on a wild goose chase.

"Not at all. She was working hard, of course, very dedicated and determined to learn everything our library had to teach her. Though, now that you mention it, perhaps she found something in one of our books and ran off to further her studies. If only we had time, I could tell you stories of my days here as a student."

"You attended school here?"

Whitmore beamed, pleased to be off the subject of Leslie Owens. "I did! Studied under Dr. Armitage himself." His smile faded. "A great loss to the school."

"Are you from the area?"

"I am," Whitmore said. "But I spent a number of years abroad to continue my studies before returning and settling down."

"You would know if anyone locally wished harm on Leslie Owens."

Whitmore's pride in his town and school served as an easy way to trip him up. He stuttered a response before blurting out, "What?

No! No one wished Miss Owens any harm." His fingers danced across the desk, fiddling with papers and pencils. "As I said, she probably ran off to research some possible discovery or rare tome without sending word to anyone. It happens more often in our department than any other."

"Students disappear without a trace often? And no one bats an eye?"

"Well, not, as you say, without a trace. No. Most of the time they turn up or send word." Whitmore grew defensive and frustrated. "We have a very dedicated student body here. Sometimes their fervor drives them into rash decisions like running off to investigate on their own. As an educator and researcher myself, I can't very well chastise them for following their passions."

"Of course not. They would have to return first."

"Exactly. Wait! I resent your implication, sir."

"What implication?"

"Well, I mean…" Whitmore grew flustered. "I'd like you to leave now. I have a great deal to accomplish before the end of the day and I can think of nothing further to offer in your efforts to locate poor Miss Owens."

"Well, thank you for your time, Professor." *Poor Miss Owens* was an interesting choice of words in the heat of the moment. "I'll be around if you think of anything more. I'm staying at the Derleth. Feel free to contact me anytime. I'll be in town for the next few days."

"Yes, of course. Good luck, sir."

"Before I go, would you happen to know anyone Leslie spent time with?"

"No, I'm sorry." Whitmore stood up to usher me out of the office. "I only spoke with her regarding academics."

"Fair enough. Again, thank you for your time."

I exited the office as the door was shoved closed behind me. I saw a flutter of fabric ripple out of sight ahead. After navigating the treacherous towers of paper crowding the narrow hallway, I found the receptionist rushing to sort through the paper and folders, eyes fixed on her desk. Walking past, I commented, "The trick is to not appear too busy or too interested in things you were ignoring when I came in."

She froze and peered up at me, eyes wide. I could see the arguments and denials forming, but only shook my head. I smiled and winked. The rising blush on her cheek revealed her embarrassment.

"You wouldn't happen to know Leslie Owens?"

"No, sorry. I don't really keep track of the students coming and going. I'm here to try to maintain the filing." She waved her hand toward the piles.

"Would they even notice if you did nothing all day?" Making sense of the chaos detailing ages long-forgotten was fighting a losing battle.

She smiled and leaned forward to whisper. "They haven't yet." She flashed a paperback book from under her desk and winked back at me.

Chuckling, I withdrew the photo of Leslie and flashed it at the receptionist. "Maybe you've seen her come by?"

"Oh, yes! A lovely young woman. She came by often. Professor Whitmore had a standing appointment with her as she worked on her research paper."

"Sounds like a dedicated teacher. Does he show the same level of interest in all his students?"

"Actually, no. He always said Leslie was a special case and needed to be guided to fulfill her potential." The receptionist leaned forward. "Or that's what I heard him say through the door." She let out a small giggle.

"Can you tell me about the last time she came in? Anything unusual about it?"

"No, nothing I can think of. She came in, met with the professor, and left like normal. Though she always would give me a small wave on her way in and out. That time, she was so deep in thought, she ignored me entirely. Her eyes were heavy as well, as if she hadn't been sleeping for days. It happens with the students, sometimes, so I didn't think much of it."

"Thanks, I'll let you get back to your... work."

"You bet. I'm just getting to the good part."

I left the department, laughing all the way down the hallway. If I had the money to hire someone to help around the office, I'd consider making her an offer.

Outside, my exhaustion hit me hard, but a hunch demanded I fight it off for a while longer. I found a spot behind the hedge line with a clear view of the front doors. Tired as I was, I suspected the professor, nervous and jittery, would panic just enough to lead me somewhere useful. If I was wrong, I'd only be out a few hours of sleep. The cold, New England air helped keep me awake while

I sat watching and waiting. When Whitmore exited, he struggled to pull his long, oversized coat over his shoulders. Preoccupied, he hurried by my hiding spot and rushed along the patchwork of angled pathways through campus. He carried an overstuffed satchel on one shoulder, which made getting his coat on even more difficult in his agitated state. I waited a beat and trailed after at a discreet distance. I could have been attached at his hip, and he would never have known with how frantically he raced away from campus.

I gambled that, as a local, he'd walk to and from work and didn't bother to retrieve my car. I didn't want to miss him leaving; I could always return the next day if I was wrong. Whitmore rushed down the darkening sidewalk, striding with the confidence of a long-time resident who knew the streets without checking a street sign or landmark. Unaccustomed to being followed, or unconcerned, Whitmore made straight for his destination. The gothic mansion he walked toward was an ornate building across the street from the Arkham Historical Society.

Whitmore passed through the black iron gates, hustled up the steps to a darkened porch, and knocked on the front door. It cracked open enough for Whitmore and another to exchange words before the former slipped in and disappeared. None of the lights so much as flickered within, making it impossible to track movement. The building sat silent and ominous as night claimed Arkham. A shiver wriggled up my spine as I stared at the building. I decided to return in the morning after a decent night's sleep. If Whitmore was warning them about me, I'd need a clear head to navigate the situation. I noted the street, South Garrison, and drew closer to read the small plaque hanging from a post embedded in the front lawn. The words on the wooden sign were carved by an expert craftsman and painted silver.

"The Silver Twilight Lodge."

The Silver Twilight Lodge

After a night plagued by dark dreams full of writhing creatures and forbidden secrets gurgled through alien lips, I made my way back to The Silver Twilight Lodge. I hammered on the door hard enough to rattle anyone inside who expected a relaxing morning. Even in the light of day, the building remained cloaked in shadows of black and grey. Tiny embellishments of silver twinkled in the darkness but only served to emphasize the unnatural gloom. The house would have been better suited as a gothic mortuary than a lodge for men to gather and get drunk. Even with the abyssal colors masking most of the features, one could spy missing shingles atop the widow's spire and dry rot creeping along the window frames.

The door swung open. An impeccably dressed man sporting a three-piece suit and gold pocket chain smiled from inside the foyer. He stood at just the right angle to block a curious visitor's prying eyes.

"May I help you?" he asked.

"You can!" I put a lot of enthusiasm into my patter, hoping to overwhelm any suspicions with chipper gullibility. "Name's Martin Williams. I'm new in town and wanted to inquire about membership. I used to belong to a chapter of the Freemasons back in New York. I haven't run across a local chapter here, so I thought I'd swing by and see if you were up for some new blood."

"Did you now?"

"Yes, sir."

"So, you aren't a..." He produced a slip of paper. "A Mr. Travis Daniels, Private Detective from New York City investigating the disappearance of one Leslie Owens?"

What the hell? Did Whitmore draw this guy a picture of me?

He continued. "I believe you spoke with one of our members last night? I understand you followed Professor Whitmore here in your boorish attempt to snoop on his movements."

The conversation with Whitmore replayed in my mind. Details like my name and city had never come up. The shifty professor had relayed our meeting to his lodge brothers. He knew more than he let on, and this place had something to do with Leslie's disappearance. Who were these people? How did this guy have information even Whitmore didn't? I had mentioned staying at the Derleth. Did someone in the Lodge with a clout call and check up on me? I *knew* there was no way anyone followed me while I tracked Whitmore, nor did the preoccupied professor notice me. I needed through the door.

"Don't bother with flashing your gun or trying to barge in, boy. There are powers far beyond anything you can muster in this reality, ready to cut you down if you do. Leave. Now."

He moved to slam the door in my face, but I reached out to hold it open. The impact stung my hand and sent a bolt of pain through my body. Through gritted teeth, I said, "Now listen old man, we can go about this privately or I can involve the police."

The doorman smirked. "Oh? Is that so? Please, come in then." He stepped aside and waved his hand in a grand gesture.

I stepped in with care, my face never leaving the amused eyes of the strange doorman. He closed the door and directed me to a side room just off the foyer, a sitting room papered in rich, red wallpaper and furnished with plush burgundy chairs. It emanated a golden glow that reflected off the dark wood floor and crown molding. A large hearth dominated the center of one wall while a case of exotic curios lined another.

"Wait here, please."

Before I could react, he slid two pocket doors closed and locked me in. I tried to pry them open. Nothing budged. I cursed my stupidity for falling prey to the grandeur of the room. The lock on the window facing the front lawn slid open, and the bottom sash lifted with ease. Escape was possible, so there was a good chance the miserable doorman just didn't want me wandering around unattended while he found someone more important to threaten. Good luck with that, buddy.

During the wait, I took the time to inspect the curios on display. Years of researching items for Madam Bina had educated me on all sorts of oddities from around the world. I found the more common items, like the bleached skeletons of small creatures. There was a human skull, crude dolls used by primitive tribes in dark corners of faraway continents, and an array of rocks and gems, some raw and multifaceted, others carved into talismans. Nothing had a label and there was no obvious door or latch allowing access to the case itself. It was as if whoever installed the case had sealed everything on the shelves from wandering hands.

The doors clicked and slid open, and two men entered. Both smiled, but these were the smiles of predators come to devour easy prey. Both wore dark suits. One appeared bulky and strong, a bruiser, steady and confident in his raw power. The other, slim and twitchy, watched me through glinting, circular glasses as if I were a thing to be analyzed and dissected. My hand slid toward my gun; then the larger of the two withdrew a wallet and flashed his shiny badge. I cursed again.

"I hear you wanted to speak with the police. I'm Chief Phillips. What can I do you for, Mr. Daniels?"

"I'm in town investigating the disappearance of Leslie Owens, which I'm sure you already know."

"I've heard." His smile never wavered. "I also heard you were moving here and wanted membership under the alias of Martin Williams."

Shit.

"I saw Professor Whitmore enter here last night after our discussion. He seemed flustered."

"Oh, you just came by to check up on him, then? That's thoughtful."

Nothing good would come from responding to his jabs, so I kept my mouth shut.

"Well, let me assure you, *Mr.* Daniels." A not-so-subtle swipe at my not being a cop or any kind of official in his town. "Whitmore, a member in good standing here and a pillar of our community, told us about your little interview." He clicked his tongue like a disappointed mother hen. "No wonder he was flustered. Finding out one of his students had disappeared and being given the impression he was under investigation. It all rattled the poor man's nerves. But I assured him you don't represent any official office and I would make it my personal business to clear this up."

"Guess there's nothing else here for me to do, then."

"Don't suppose there is." Philips stepped up to me and wrapped an arm around my shoulders, guiding me toward the open doors into the hallway. "So, how long are you planning to stay in Arkham, Daniels? Staying at the Derleth, right?"

"The Derleth, yeah." No point in lying about what he already knew. "Don't know for how long."

"Well, you make sure to see the sights before you head out tomorrow. I'm sure old Belknap at the front desk won't begrudge refunding a day or two if you feel the need to leave early. And if you have any more questions, don't hesitate to visit me down at the station."

"Of course, sir."

"Good. Good. Have a wonderful visit, *Mr.* Daniels."

The door slammed closed behind me as I descended the stairs and made my way toward the sidewalk. I gave the building one last look before walking away. One of the curtains in the widow's tower rustled. With a member like the chief of police, there was no way to gain access to the building through legal recourse. Being a known entity in town didn't help, either. I considered my options and settled on checking the local hospital for any Jane Does. Maybe I'd get lucky and be able to leave the overcast town behind before Chief Phillips lost patience.

St. Mary's Hospital

The whitewashed walls of St. Mary's Hospital shimmered with the antiseptic glow of every other hospital. Doctors and nurses filled the halls with the hectic energy of purpose and importance. A desk occupied by a stern nurse dominated the center of activity. She organized and handed out papers and clipboards as if she had more than just the two hands she'd been born with. Many of the doctors who crossed by the desk accepted the orders she handed out as if they were stone tablets dictated by God.

I waited for a lull in activity before approaching the desk and flashing a smile. Her stony glare signaled all attempts at charm were destined to fail. Instead, I withdrew a fake NYPD badge and flashed it at her. "Detective Daniels, ma'am. I hate to bother you, but I'm here investigating a disappearance. I need any information you have on a Leslie Owens, a student of Miskatonic, or any Jane Does that may have come across your desk in the last few weeks."

"We're very busy, officer." She spoke through pursed lips, begrudging every word.

"I see that. Seems this place would descend into chaos without you here to direct traffic."

A little of the tension melted from her long-etched grimace, allowing some of the deep lines in her skin to relax for an instant.

"You have no idea." I offered a small, understanding nod, not pressing for help, afraid she might go on the defensive and demand a warrant I didn't have. I needed to appear as a fellow soldier, sympathetic to the plight of another beholden to fools who made far too much money. She sighed and asked, "A young girl's gone missing?"

"For a couple of weeks now, yes."

"Why is the NYPD all the way up in Massachusetts? Shouldn't the local police be investigating?"

"Influential family." I shrugged. "Local PD didn't seem concerned or interested?" It was a gamble, but after meeting the chief of police, an educated gamble.

"That about says it…" The nurse motioned one of the younger girls over, muttered some directions about who got what clipboard, and waved for me to follow.

She led me down hallways that all looked alike until we descended a flight of stairs into another series of hallways. I lost any sense of where we were within the sterile building. Her heels clicked like a severe metronome demanding a perfect tempo. A pair of metal doors banged open at the nurse's touch to reveal the records room. An elderly lady sat behind a desk, dozing in the silence of the lower level.

"Mrs. Shetly!"

The old woman stirred and glanced around. Unconcerned to be found sleeping at her post, she asked, "Yes?"

"This detective requires access to our records for an investigation. Please provide him with whatever he needs." She nodded to me and left with absolute certainty her orders would be followed.

"What are you looking for, Detective?"

"I need information about a Leslie Owens or Jane Does from the last couple weeks."

The woman nodded. Her eyes drooped as if still weighed down by sleep, reluctant to be roused from whatever dream they'd entertained. She groaned to her feet and shuffled off into the rows of shelves lined with color-coded files. I glanced into the hallway, checking to see if anyone had come to greet the out-of-town police officer, specifically a police chief coming to interfere with said "officer's" efforts. Nothing stirred in the underbelly of the hospital. A cloud of general malaise hung over the quiet corridor. In the quiet, I had a moment to recognize the same undercurrent of unease had drifted through the main floors but was masked by the flurry of activity. Come to think of it, I didn't remember seeing any patients being transported or family walking through the halls. Only staff.

Mrs. Shetly interrupted my thoughts by dropping a substantial stack of files on her desk. "I didn't see anything for a Leslie Owens. No Owens at all, in fact. Here are all the Jane Does from the last two weeks, though."

I ran my finger along the side of the towering pile. "This is two weeks of Jane Does?" There had to be more than sixty files.

She shrugged as if it was normal. "We get a lot of John and Jane Does. Mostly every patient here is designated Doe, really."

I hefted the pile to an empty bench and began sifting through the files, searching for any descriptions matching Leslie. With any luck, I could pare the pile down to a manageable size.

Only three files came close to describing Leslie. Two of the women remained in the hospital, both comatose. The third had been released into the care of a Dr. Norman Mintz. I copied the necessary information into my notebook and handed the pile back to Mrs. Shetly.

"Thank you. Could you tell me how to find these patients?" I showed Mrs. Shetly the two names of the girls still on-site.

"Take the elevator to the second and fifth floors," she said after checking the relevant files.

"And where can I find Dr. Mintz's office?"

"He's the administrator at the Sanitarium across the river."

"Thanks."

The hallways stretched into eternity, interrupted by the occasional T-section. After walking for what felt like the length of numerous football fields, I found a sign directing me to an elevator. On the second and fifth floors, I still found only staff rushing along. None of them paid me any attention. I had the room numbers of the two patients in my notebook and avoided any additional attention by keeping my head down and acting as if I belonged. Neither patient matched my picture of Leslie, so that left the one under Mintz's care.

As I made my way back to the elevator, I peered into the rooms I passed. Every patient lay in a comatose state. I watched the doctors and nurses race along the hallways, yet not once did any of them enter a room to check on their patients. I decided to snoop a bit more, never moving too far from the elevators, fearful of getting lost and discovering more comatose patients.

On the way down, I stopped on the fourth and third floors. On both, I found more of the same. Comatose patients lay in their beds as busy staff raced by the rooms, never entering. Everyone just seemed to be running in circles, shuffling papers, and barking orders no one paid any heed to. Once on the ground floor, I rushed to the front lobby, desperate to escape the hospital before the endless halls could claim me like the army of doctors and nurses who never accomplished anything substantive. On crossing the main desk, I caught the eye of the nurse and offered a curt nod. She stared back. A twinge of confusion crossed her scrunched features. She either didn't recognize me or hadn't expected to see me again after dropping me off in the records room.

Once outside, back under the perpetual shadows of the Arkham streets, I took a deep breath. I headed to the sanitorium, glad to put as much distance between myself and the unnaturally quiet hospital.

Arkham Sanitarium

Walking down Pickman Street on the way to the sanitarium gave me time to consider the situation. If I found Leslie Owens locked away in the local mental hospital, her mind shattered, that would bring my investigation to its conclusion. I could stop in Bolton on my way back home to New York, tell the family, pay my debt to the Agostino Family, and move on with my life. However, if she turned out to be a victim of mental instability, how had she remained undiscovered for two weeks? Why would everyone conceal her whereabouts? And why did the teacher involve the chief of police? Nothing about this case or town made sense.

As I turned onto Peabody Avenue to retrieve my car, an itch, one I'd come to trust without question, worried at my subconscious. A glance confirmed the presence of a car parked across from mine with two men in the cab. I watched from the corner. They didn't move to get out or start their car to leave. Small-town cops stood out like a marching band when they tried to act covert. They remained in their car, chatting, and looked over at my car every few minutes. *They must not be used to stakeouts*, I thought when they didn't notice my freeze at the corner. I doubled back, unwilling to tangle with local law more than necessary. Chief Phillips must have assigned some of his boys to me to complicate my life. Why were they so concerned with me looking for a missing young woman?

I made my way down Walnut Street toward the river. My well-abused map indicated the sanitarium lay on the other side of town. The prospect of walking didn't leave me enthused, but with the police watching my car, I didn't have much choice. After two blocks, I turned on Peabody again, well out of sight of the stakeout. Ahead was an old, cramped potter's field filled with ruined crosses. It was the first spot in the dismal town I found bathed in sunlight. The crosses leaned on the verge of collapse, sometimes making it difficult to know which marker belonged to which grave. Critters scurried along the ground like dried, wind-blown leaves. A crooked tree with two long, wretched limbs reached out over the graves, both protective and covetous. The ends of the branches scratched and nudged the crosses like a patient puppeteer.

My pace quickened until the burial grounds and its botanical caretaker vanished from sight, and I was surrounded by local businesses and riverside warehouses. Even in this part of town, few residents ventured out to run errands or window shop. Walking through the streets felt like being in a world of desperate eyes peering out from the darkness, all too scared to enter open spaces, yet too curious to bury their heads in ignorance. On all sides, curtains fluttered, and the muffled tintinnabulation of tiny bells marked the entrance and exit of customers. No matter where I looked, I found nothing but the echoes of ghosts.

I hurried over the bridge as the dark waters rippled beneath. The hypnotic glimmer of rushing water hid the strong undercurrent waiting to swallow the unwary. A ferry idled down the river, passing beneath the bridge. Groups of figures draped in dark, wet raincoats lurched along the deck. One looked up at the bridge. Our eyes locked. I gasped at the visage of the barely humanoid patron with bulging eyes, thin lips, and too-flat features. I raced to the sanitarium as gurgled laughter from the receding figure merged with the lapping waves like two instruments from the same orchestra.

No longer daring to scan my surroundings, I focused on getting to the sanitarium and finding Leslie in order to escape the damned town. As Arkham Sanitarium came into view, the differences between this forbidding fortress and St. Mary's were clear. The hospital presented a facade of clean normality on the outside. The sanitarium sported tall towers that blocked the horizon along the crenelated walls. White-dressed men, guards, and nurses passed the glass windows, patrolling the inner halls like soldiers out of a medieval fantasy. The tall, wrought-iron gates enclosed a vast, green field that wrapped around the sprawling building.

The large front gates creaked in a light breeze, open to any who wished entrance or escape. I slipped through, keeping an eye out for security or a roaming, disturbed patient and cut a path across the wide, empty lawn. As if unconcerned with who might be foolish enough to gain entrance to the sanitarium, not a single security guard arrived to question my presence. For a brief second, I questioned my own existence; nothing about my visit to Arkham had matched my expectations or experiences.

I climbed the dingy, cracked steps and pulled open the paint-chipped front door. The walls of the sanitarium were a sickening greenish-yellow, either from age or mold. My shoes squelched with every sticky step. The lime green linoleum floor was covered in unidentifiable dark green and brown speckles. A nurse stood in the hallway, smoking a cigarette, gazing into nothing. As the screams of patients bounced against the walls to create a symphony of anguish and insanity, she took a calm drag, oblivious to the wretchedness around her. The smell of nicotine mixed with the aroma of urine, vomit, and the putrid odor of rotting seafood. With a handkerchief balled up and pressed to my face, I approached the bored, laconic nurse.

"Can you direct me to a Dr. Mintz?"

Her eyes twitched toward me long enough to point down the hall with her chin. Rather than waste time attempting to converse with the disinterested healthcare worker, I strode down the hall searching for someone more animated and helpful. As I grew used to the smell, the handkerchief disappeared into my pocket. My steps clicked along the hallway. In direct contradiction to the hospital, no one hustled through these hallways. Expecting to see male nurses wrestling with unruly patients or drooling residents giggling in corners, I found only the gibbering of madness muffled behind metal doors and plaster walls.

A wooden door with a frosted glass window came into view. The name "Dr. Charles Mintz" was painted onto the glass. My knocking reverberated down the hallway, setting off a wave of mad screams that folded into the already nerve-wracking din. A voice from within the office bade me enter. Sitting behind an expensive, dark, wood desk was the bespectacled man from the Silver Twilight Lodge who had accompanied Chief Phillips. A sly hyena smile stretched across his pale face.

"Mr. Daniels! I am surprised to see you here. To what do I owe the pleasure?"

I considered lying, but knew it wouldn't hold up. Screw it. Best to let them know I'm not giving up and to hell with their threats. "I found a record suggesting someone matching Leslie Owens's description was checked out of St. Mary's by you. I came to ask about it."

"It's not uncommon for us to take possession of cases presenting mental instability from the hospital, but I don't recall admitting a Leslie Owens."

"She was admitted as a Jane Doe. I came to see if I could confirm her identity."

"I see. Do you have the case number?"

I recited the number I'd copied from the St. Mary's file. He nodded and walked over to a series of file cabinets and began riffling through the files. "I apologize for Phillips at the Lodge. He is territorial, and our doorman informed us a deranged individual had appeared. We came expecting a fiend jumping around, wrecking our sitting room." He cackled at his own words as he withdrew a folder from the drawer. "This should be it. Let's have a look, shall we?" He flipped through, reading his notes. "Yes, I know of this young woman. She is suffering from a severe psychosis. She's scheduled for electro-shock right now. Come, I'll walk you down."

The doctor flopped the file onto his desk and motioned for the door. He hummed a jaunty tune ill-fit for the depressed atmosphere. We descended two floors via a narrow flight of stairs. He pushed open a heavy, rusted door, revealing a dark tunnel. Weak bulbs were mounted to the wall along a frayed electrical system; one bad spark and the whole building would go up, killing everyone.

We entered a portion of the sanitarium better described as a subterranean cave system. Copper pipes and thick bundles of wiring ran the length of the worn stone walls and ceiling. Lightbulbs meant to illuminate the stubborn darkness did nothing more than create a series of middling spotlights along the tunnel. I looked back at the stairwell made of plaster and concrete to assure myself I hadn't somehow stepped into the Dark Ages.

"This is a dungeon."

"Used to be, actually. This land belonged to one of the founding families of Arkham. Rather than remodel, we just ran some necessities down here. It was cheap and efficient. Two of any government's favorite words. This way." Mintz sped down the tunnel until he reached a rusted, but solid, door. He unlocked it with a large skeleton key attached to a massive ring looped to his belt. It was the kind of keyring you'd expect to see a jailor carry on his person. As the door squealed open, the doctor motioned. "After you, Mr. Daniels."

"You first, Doctor."

Mintz grinned as he lifted his hand and snapped his fingers. Amplified by the underground acoustics, the crisp sound filled the tunnel. Before I could react, an enormous hand reached out of the room and grabbed my shoulder. It dragged me in as a second hand clamped down on my other arm to stop me from reaching for my gun. A dull-eyed behemoth of a man lifted me into the air, squeezing my lungs like a near-empty tube of toothpaste.

Mintz tittered from the doorway. "We can't have you poking around, Mr. Daniels. You should have left when you had the chance."

As the iron grip tightened, compressing my lungs to pulp, my vision grew dark. I swung my head back and drove it forward, smashing my forehead into the brute's emotionless face. A wet crunch coupled with a surprised grunt led to my attacker releasing me. I crumbled to the ground but managed to draw my revolver and level it against the barrel-chested giant. Three shots sent him staggering back before he dropped to the ground like a chopped tree. I turned my aim toward the door, expecting to find the good doctor, but he'd already fled.

"Damn it."

Thankfully, he'd panicked and forgot to lock the cell door.

A horrid stench arose out of nowhere. After being crushed by the brute's inhuman grasp, I sucked down enormous, ragged breaths. A putrid morass filled my mouth, throat, and lungs. I coughed from the fight, the odor befuddling my mind. I pulled the handkerchief out, bundled the fabric over my nose and mouth, and searched for the source of the sudden fetor. Lying dead on the floor, my once enormous assailant dissolved into a bubbling purple-red ichor streaked with thick, black ooze.

A trickle of moisture dribbled down my forehead. I reached up with the handkerchief to wipe away what I assumed was sweat, but found the cloth smeared with the same thick, black substance. I tossed the handkerchief away and scanned the room for a towel or rag. It was lined with plastic drop sheets for easy clean-up after the thing melting on the floor had finished with me. I fled the room, removed the spent casings from my revolver with shaking hands, and struggled to reload. With my gun ready, I took a shuddered breath and retraced our path through the mildew-slick tunnel to the stairs leading back to the main hallway.

An eerie silence replaced the unending screams from before. No one came to investigate or stop me as I made my way back to the doctor's office. All the doors of the sanitarium were open, and the rooms sat empty. No nurses, orderlies, or guards patrolled the hallways. It was abandoned.

Mintz's door was open, his office ransacked. The folder he'd consulted earlier was gone, his drawers flung open and emptied. Regardless of the mess, I sifted through the papers. Page after discarded page, nothing indicated or even hinted at his or the Lodge's plans. An envelope poked out from under one of the cabinets. I fished it out and found it postmarked from New York City. I withdrew the letter and gave it a cursory scan. As the words formed sentences, a mixture of anger and dread crept into my gut like someone had purchased my future grave for the sole purpose of walking over it several hundred times.

"To the Members of the Silver Twilight Lodge:

I'm sure your little group of miscreants are responsible for the kidnapping of the Owens child, my niece. Do not think this pathetic action will force me to surrender the text you desire. The girl means little to me and will in no way advance your schemes or prove a hindrance to my plans. Still, this insult cannot go unanswered. Release the child or suffer a fate far worse than anything you might inflict against the girl.

Remember your oaths. The Elder Ones do not forgive treachery or suffer those who overstep themselves. Their terrible and obedient shoggoths are forever hungry.

Ph'nglui Mglw'nafh Cthulhu R'lyeh wgah'nagl fhyagn.

Sir Edward Martin Mandeville"

I folded the letter and stuffed it into my pocket, too frustrated to preserve its condition. Despite avoiding the gang wars of New York City, I'd somehow been thrust into the middle of a battle between two groups, both of which were deep into a kind of weirdness beyond my understanding. Mandeville had flashed a pile of money and pointed me like a gun, or worse, a sacrificial distraction. The girl's retrieval seemed to be of no importance to the old bastard. If she came out of this whole, it might mitigate Mandeville's response. One way or the other, the letter made it clear a response was coming.

I struggled with the decision to abandon the case and girl or see it through. On one hand, this whole situation proved to be more complicated and far stranger than anything I'd ever been involved with. On the other hand, there was the life of an innocent girl in the balance, and neither of the primary parties seemed to care about her safety. She still had parents waiting at home. People who loved her. The stuffy room weighed down on me as I pondered the two sides and my moral obligations. With a flip of a small metal latch, I unlocked the window and lifted it to let in some fresh air.

As the window rose, a gust of stagnant air evacuated the room, and a fresh breeze rushed in. I took a deep breath, eyes closed and head pressed against the cool glass. A faint odor of rot and medicine intruded into the office like a harbinger of doom. I turned around, my gun drawn, expecting another of Mintz's brutes. The office remained empty, but the faint smell lingered. Some papers on the floor fluttered under the influence of a stream of air flowing from behind the file cabinet where I'd found the letter.

I grabbed the cabinet and tossed it aside, sending papers and folders billowing. Beneath, a gaping hole awaited, black and forbidding. Metal rungs secured into the concrete foundation descended into darkness. A strange fetid odor, similar to the stench wafting off the dead brute, pumped out of the abyssal depths like the steam from city subway lines. Moist gusts pulsed from the hole as if the lungs of the Earth labored below the sanitarium. During a pause in the steady, titanic surges of hot air, a faint whimper traveled through the unseen underground pathways.

I wanted to ignore that simple sound. I wanted to turn away and run back to New York City. Instead, without thinking, I rushed to the desk, found a stray flashlight, and began climbing down those grimy metal rungs into the darkness below.

The Laboratory

The foundation transitioned to solid rock as I descended deeper into the pit. Once my feet touched the roughhewn floor of the tunnel, I switched on the flashlight. Holding my revolver out in front of me, I crossed my wrists to keep the light and the gun aimed together. Moisture glistened over the jagged rock walls. The thunderous roar of rushing air sent a layer of grit dancing to the ground, yet the tunnel was devoid of even a faint breeze.

The whimpering grew louder as I traversed the uneven tunnel. Forced to squeeze through tight sections, my suit caught and tore often. I ignored the destruction of my clothing and followed the twisting, erratic path until I came to a stone portal leading into a wide cavern. I stepped inside. It stretched beyond what I could see with the flashlight, but the walls were lined with gas lamps. I found a switch, turned off my flashlight, and flipped it.

The lamps flared to life, revealing three operating tables stained with gore and chemicals. A horrid rainbow of red, yellow, green, and brown mapped unspeakable horrors committed under the flickering gas lamps. Like a macabre multi-colored Rorschach test, a parade of nightmare imaginings marched through my mind with each new splatter. A cart near the tables glittered with surgical tools and butcher knives. All showed signs of use from Dr. Mintz's nefarious and demented work. Shelves of chemicals lined the wall to the left. Larger, clouded canisters filled with obscured contents resembling bits of the vile creatures I'd seen depicted in the mural on the university library ceiling lined the right.

The back of the room was pocketed with a series of cells, either natural or carved, secured with thick iron bars. None of the gas lamps shed a sliver of light into any of them. Figures shuffled in the darkness, retreating farther into their confinement as I approached. One of the occupants inched closer, limping as if hobbled. A series of gurgling, wet attempts at speech beckoned me closer.

Unsure what new horror the doctor had conjured or inflicted, I steadied myself and my revolver against whatever I would discover and flicked on the flashlight.

The huddled prisoner turned away from the sudden blast of light, covering their face. Shrouded in a dirt-encrusted burlap robe, they showed subtle signs of the misdeeds carved into them. Aspects of their cloaked anatomy didn't match up with the human form. A strange writhing rippled beneath the thick, coarse robe. I dismissed it as a trick of the light and pervasive shadows. I *had* to dismiss it before my mind snapped.

"Where is the key to the cells? I'll get you out and to a hospital. I'm here looking for a girl Mintz kidnapped and brought here. Have you seen a young girl?"

A water-clogged groan bubbled from under the bundle of rags, followed by a wet flop as the heap lurched closer to the bars. The improvised hood slipped off the prisoner, revealing the abomination. Staring at the monstrosity drawing closer, I froze under a terror I'd never experienced before or since. My body refused to move. I couldn't hear my heart as it raced to break free of my chest and flee. Only the desperate groan of the creature broke through my brittle sanity. Air wouldn't flow into my lungs. A cloud of miasma rose from the ichor that oozed with every step the creature suffered.

Its mouth tore open, revealing a toothy, gnashing maw. A slime-coated tentacle slithered through the bars. Pure, mindless instinct forced my muscles into action. I stumbled back, fell to the ground, and used my palms and heels to skitter away from the reaching appendage. A dissonance of watery bleats filled the air. More writhing tendrils emerged from the other cells; all the creatures pressed up against the bars, reaching out, searching. The squeals grew frantic and agitated. Bowels filled with ice, I retreated to the medical tables, smashing the cart of razor-sharp tools to the ground. I scrambled away from the rain of metal and collided with a workstation, heedless of chemicals being tipped over and spilled to the ground. An unsteady metal scraping and clicking broke me out of my panic. My hands were empty. I patted my barren holster before turning.

One of the tentacles had my revolver. The creature fumbled with the gun, trying to turn the muzzle against itself, but its slime-covered appendages were incapable of maneuvering the weapon enough to use it. Its whines turned to anguish as it released the gun, letting it fall to the ground. Despondent, enraged, the beast roared, slamming tentacles and its own body against the cage and walls. Wails exploded from the other cells. Agitated by the first creature's outburst, other equally monstrous beings lashed out against their cells. The urge to leave the gun behind, run back to New York, and drown my memories of Arkham in many bottles of alcohol dragged me to my feet. Before I could follow through, the first creature wrapped its appendages around the bars and dragged itself forward. Between two of the bars, I stared into a single, scared, brown human eye.

I walked over the scattered bric-a-brac, careful to avoid dangerous liquids, and upturned scalpels knocked to the ground during my thrashing retreat. A dirty rag hung from the edge of one of the examination tables. Ignoring the stains, forcing my mind not to linger on anything in the room around me, I slid the gun away from the creature. That eye never flickered. It begged for mercy without saying a single word. I met the gaze of all the prisoners who struggled to drag, hop, lurch, slither, and tumble to the bars. Confronted by forms twisted and mutated beyond comprehension, their eyes retained the last shred of humanity they were able to cling to. Every one of those souls screamed out for a mercy Mintz would never grant.

When I walked out of the room, it smelled of sulfur, reflecting the hell on earth it had become. This hell, however, was empty of demons and damned souls. The spent cartridges fell out of the cylinder, tinging like tiny bells as they hit the gravel-covered floor. A bottle of liquid that smelled like gasoline poured out a trail behind me. Before ascending the ladder, I refilled the chambers and snapped the gun closed. I thought for a moment about putting the gun to my head, desperate to eradicate the memories of what had happened in the room. Instead, I found a match in my pocket, lit it, and flicked it at the thin trail of chemicals. It ignited a light blue and raced away toward the lab.

Back in the doctor's office, I caught a reflection in the window as night fell over Arkham. The face staring out from the shadowed glass was haunted and exhausted. Too much seen in the bowels of the Earth. Too much learned in the short time since he'd left New York. As the horrors wriggled in a nightmarish dance through his mind, tears streamed down that man's face.

The first rumbling explosion reverberated through the sanitarium and broke me out of my reverie. I swallowed the unbidden cackle fighting its way up my throat. If I let it loose, I would never stop. My life would be defined by someone pumping me full of meds, electro-shocks, and a world no larger than a small cell in this or some other house of madness and misery.

The vision of sticky tentacles, throbbing pustules, and sad, lidless eyes forever staring out at a world they could never be a part of again brought me to my knees. My stomach expelled tangy bile and acid. I wiped my mouth across a tattered sleeve and made for the exit. The underground rumbles of explosions followed me into the cool night air.

No one walked the streets of Arkham. Nothing stood in my path. Nothing dared.

Where Truth Meets Madness

A bruised horizon outlined the strange angles of Arkham's skyline. The grounds of the sanitarium lay empty and quiet. A cold breeze whispered across tufts of grass. From a distance, the city appeared quiet, peaceful. My march back through town passed in a blur of disassociation. Nothing felt real as the cross streets glided by and lights in the windows flickered on and off. Whispers, rustling footsteps, and rattling growls dogged my every step, yet I remained focused on the path ahead. The gun dangled from my fist. One finger tapped the side of the trigger, ready for the next abomination to emerge from the inky darkness.

The police stakeout remained parked farther up the street when I reached my car. I ignored them and got in, pushed the starter paddle, and slammed on the gas. They followed me to the city limits, but no farther. The night grew darker, more sinister. The road stretched out into eternity, promising life, death, oblivion, and answers I didn't want to know but still needed. The fields flashed by. Inhuman shadows crawled and twitched under the cover of a moonless night. Winged creatures cavorted with spindle-legged monstrosities. Alien howls filled the air, withering into distant moans as I cruised onward.

As the sun crested the horizon, the writhing beasts evaporated like mist. I knew they'd return as soon as the glorious, unforgiving sun dipped below the other side of the rational world. My hope was to be done with all this by then, one way or another. Trailing a storm of dust behind, I tore through downtown Bolton. The two checkers-playing old-timers remained fixed over their board, paying no attention to the lunatic racing through their town. At the home of the Owens, I skidded to a stop and got out. I marched up to the front door and drove my foot into the space near the knob. I knew how to shatter a sturdy door with the right amount of force and proper aim. This one would have yielded to a strong breeze. The weather-beaten wood exploded inward, sending splinters flying, and left ragged slats swinging on loose hinges.

Mr. and Mrs. Owens remained on their dusty couch, staring at the wall as the paper crumbled and snowed to the floor. They didn't react to the door being broken down or to the deranged detective barging into their home. Mrs. Owens spoke in a droning voice devoid of any emotion. "Detective, we didn't expect you back."

"I want answers."

"We told you what we could," Mr. Owens said.

"Well, it wasn't enough! Who is the Silver Twilight Lodge? Why are they trying to blackmail Mandeville with your daughter's life? What the hell is going on?"

Their heads swiveled in unison toward me. Speaking in synch with one another in a haunting, inhuman voice that shook the small room, they intoned, "The girl is special. The first daughter in more than one hundred generations. She will bring forth the New Dawn. She will end the long twilight."

It was like hearing a radio broadcast overlaid with the same content repeated by a multitude of disparate voices.

Both Owenses began convulsing. Blood dripped from their eyes, mouths, noses, and ears. They fell from the couch to the floor. Reacting without thought, I rushed to Mrs. Owens' side and lifted her lithe, wasted form into my arms. Thinking to bring them both to a hospital, I attempted to carry her out the front door. At the threshold, a force pressed against us, refusing to let her body out of the house. A loud series of bangs echoed from upstairs as all the doors slammed open at the same time.

A chorus of agitated chittering rattled from above and behind me. I turned just enough to find the upstairs landing swallowed by an eternity of purple haze and black cosmos. Ancient lifeforms floated in the endless empty. Some were eons away and others a mere ten feet up rickety stairs. The hungry, ravening increased as the eternal nothing crept closer to consume us.

Fed up with the strange powers stacked against me, I gritted my teeth and pushed harder. Mrs. Owens screamed a shrill, painful wail that grew with intensity as I inched through the confining force. As if stretched too far like a rubber band, the force snapped, and an eerie purple aura crackled around Mrs. Owens. I passed through the door as a ghostly purple entity was ripped from her body. Its ghostly face, twisted in pain, shuddered as I stepped onto the porch.

The ephemeral form dissipated into nothingness as it continued a horrible, silent scream. I took Mrs. Owens to the car and helped her into the passenger seat. Before I could return to rescue Mr. Owens, the house ignited under a curtain of purple and green flames. The rotted roof caved in, and walls broke apart, decaying into dust within seconds. The fire wasn't consuming the house so much as aging it. The entropy of decades occurred before my eyes in seconds. Mr. Owens' body, visible through a cracked window, crumbled into a skeleton, then into dust.

A cough from my car brought me back to Mrs. Owens' side. She reached out, grasping at the air. I took her hand and assured her, "I'll get you to a hospital."

She shook her head. "No time. I'm dying. Part of the curse Uncle Mandeville put on us for losing Leslie."

"I'll kill that old bastard!"

"No." Mrs. Owens' grip tightened. "He'd destroy you. Hide her." She coughed up a glob of phlegmy blood. Small maggots squirmed in the residue. I choked down my own bile. Mrs. Owens continued speaking, ignoring her obvious pain. "Listen! We didn't know Leslie had disappeared until Mandeville called us."

"Wait, *he* called *you*?"

"Yes, he knew she'd vanished and began calling us, demanding to know where she was and why we hadn't stopped her from leaving for college. When he discovered she'd not only gone off to school but that she was doing research at Miskatonic University, he became furious. He screamed a series of words we didn't understand. By the end of the day, we'd been confined to the house and possessed by some kind of alien beings made of pure energy." She coughed, spitting up more blood and maggots. "You aren't the first person he's sent to investigate this. You have to be careful."

"How many before me?"

"Four others. I don't think any of them got out of Arkham."

There had been four of those abominations in the laboratory. Had that been my future? I felt nausea rising once more. Mrs. Owens tugged at my arm, forcing my focus back onto her. Strength faded from her body. She whispered, "You're a distraction. They all were. Mandeville is using you. He only needs to keep the Lodge busy while he prepares. Detective, please find my little girl and run! He can't be allowed to have her."

"Prepare for what?"

"His retribution."

"Come on, I'll get you down to Boston where someone can patch you up."

Mrs. Owens pushed herself past me and out of the car. She crawled across the dry, cracked dirt surrounding the rubble of her home. "I won't make it. I can feel things eating away at my insides. Go. Save Leslie."

I withdrew my gun and offered it to her.

"No, Mr. Daniels. Thank you, but no." She scanned the flat, empty land stretching out around her. "This used to be a wonderful community, full of life. A pestilence unlike anything we'd seen before ruined all of that. We burned it all to the ground and salted our own land to stop it from spreading." She coughed again before vomiting up a thick sludge of clotted blood swarming with pale, squirming larvae. "It's an odd thing to sacrifice so much to save a world that will never know how close it came to destruction." She offered a final, blood-tinged smile before lying down in the dust and watching the sky as her breaths came slower. "Goodbye, Mr. Daniels. Tell my Leslie her parents loved her."

"I will, ma'am."

My car rolled out of that dust-lined town for the last time as I headed back to Arkham. God help me, as if that was still an option.

Arkham, Massachusetts

The streets of Arkham, although never very populated, were devoid of any living creatures as dusk fell over the city. No window shades rustled as my car rolled past. No cars, no people, no wind, no sound traveled the byways of Arkham save for me. I pulled up to the Derleth, parked, and entered. The front lobby sat empty as if abandoned for decades. No longer surprised by the ominous tendencies of the town, I made my way up to my room. Everything I'd left behind waited for my uncertain return. I changed out of the tattered remnants of my suit, got a quick shower, and put on a clean set of clothes. I was sure they would be soiled by morning. I reloaded my gun, pocketed as many bullets as I could, and made my way back to those infernal streets.

The walk to the Lodge was like drifting through a dream. Every step sounded muffled and soft, as if the world were real and the surreal all at once. By the time I reached the Lodge, a starless, moonless night had claimed the town. No lights shined through the many windows glaring out over the world. An aura of shimmering darkness hovered over the surface of the ornate building. I made my way around the property, searching for alternate access, covert enough to avoid alerting anyone too soon. Crisp, dry leaves crumpled under my feet like a natural alarm system. It was as if nature itself were against me. Maybe it was. The plan was to find the girl, sneak out, and run. Anyone or anything in the way would have to kill me to stop me. If I wanted to survive, however, it would be better to avoid the Lodge Members and Mandeville, if the old man showed up.

None of the windows or doors eased open. Along the base of the house, a small window peeked out from the foundation. Up close, through the cloudy, unwashed glass, I could make out the milky outlines of boxes stacked in a far corner of what appeared to be a cellar. I placed my jacket over the glass and used the grip of my revolver to smash it in. The jacket muffled the sound outside, but did nothing for the falling shards within. After a slow count of ten, no one appeared to investigate. I cleared the rest of the glass from the frame and, shaking out stray shards of glass from my jacket, shimmied through the opening.

Glass crunched under my weight as I dropped to the floor. Musty and damp, the cellar came into focus as my eyes adjusted to the new level of darkness. Moldering boxes sat on top of iron-banded crates. The bands were an inch thick and showed signs of rust. Brushing a layer of dust away revealed faint etchings of what I assumed to be runes. One of the etchings nicked my skin. A small bead of blood rose on my finger, which I sucked on while exploring the rest of the room.

A door stood on the far side, visible through a crack in the many towering rows of boxes and crates. A rumpled pile of discarded clothes lay to one side of the door. New, clean fabric lay atop older, moth-eaten rags. Lifting a layer to see underneath released a wave of foul air contaminated with rot and mold. Bits of moist, decaying fabric clung to my hand as I backed away. I dragged my palm against the chilled stone wall. A coating of thin slime clung to my hand, which I wiped against my trousers. Before cracking open the door and peeking through, I withdrew my gun.

At the end of an indistinct space, another door glowed with soft red-orange light around the edges. The glow revealed the outline of stairs climbing up into the main house. A combination of noises, splitting wood and whining metal, pulled my attention away from the door. From the iron-bound crate rose a hulking, grey figure. Larger than Gargantua the gorilla from the traveling Ringling Bros. Circus, the malformed creature kicked the remnants of the crate aside with one of its great webbed feet. Yellowed fangs poked out of his grimacing maw. Small, black eyes glinted from beneath the ripple of drooping skin that served as a brow. Overlong arms hung at its side. Flexing both fists, it tested its newfound freedom. Standing there, gaping at the monstrosity before me, I struggled to bring my gun to bear.

The creature reached down, lifted a broken shard of metal, and launched it at me. I dove into the pile of rotten clothes just before the metal cut the air above me and thunked into the door. As the monster stomped closer, I rolled from the clothes and found my gun three feet away, dropped during my desperate leap. As I scrambled across the floor to retrieve my weapon, a heavy hand slammed down on my back, pushing all air and sense out of me. Cool and damp, like a creature emerging from a humid marsh, the enormous hand lifted my body from the ground only to slam me into the wall beside the door. The metal shard still vibrated from the impact and buzzed in my ear.

The face, grey and snarling, stared through me with alien eyes as its grip tightened. Desperate, I reached out and fumbled with the metal shard. Jagged edges sliced deep into my palms, blood coating the metal and ruining my tenuous hold. Pain jolted through my hands as my fingers tightened around the shard. As everything grew fuzzy and a final black fog stole my vision, I jerked and ripped the metal from the door, stabbing it at the creature. The metal pierced its face with a vile squelch. My vision faded, and I thought the monster impervious to my attack. A strangled croak gave me reason to hope.

The grip slackened. As I sucked in air made putrid with the smell and taste of rotting fish, my burning lungs accepted the reprieve with little complaint. I stared at the dead creature as it lay at my feet, the metal shard jammed deep into what appeared to be gills. I recovered my gun and, with a final glance at the dead creature, left it behind and limped toward the glowing door.

Gun outstretched before me, I cleared the stairs to make sure no one or no thing waited to pounce from above. Low, murmured chanting pulsed through the closed door. I gripped the doorknob. Heat radiated through the wood, and my every breath became more difficult than the one before.

The door swung open on smooth, whispering hinges. Amber light flooded out, forcing me to squint. Once I adjusted to the blazing light, a massive, circular room with an impossible ceiling reaching into infinity came into focus. A series of symbols and runes were carved into the floor, creating numerous interwoven geometric patterns. A snaking scrawl of unreadable, writhing text encircled the designs. At the center stood a young woman gagged and tied to a pillar made of dark metal covered with glowing red veins that sprouted from the ground. Dark hair, bright eyes, and a button nose. Leslie Owens.

Terror-born tears streamed from her bloodshot eyes. Two shots rang out before I realized I'd taken aim at the two nearest chanters. They crumbled to the floor, but it did nothing to stop the others in the throes of their ceremony. I fired two more shots and dropped two more chanters. One of the cultists stepped forward, holding a small idol in the shape of a slender barrel with upside-down crescent wings unfurled from the center of its back. Instead of a head, there appeared to be a blossoming flower with fleshy petals. The petals were lined with filaments or teeth and long eye stalks sprouted from the middle. Webbed appendages formed curved arms and legs. As the statue was brought closer to Leslie, she screamed through the tight gag. The leader raised the statue to the ceiling and called out an impossible name. The statue was pressed into Leslie's belly as the leader whispered a strange phrase I recognized from the end of Mandeville's letter. Afterward, he set the idol on the floor, out of the reach of her thrashing feet.

The cultists all took up the name that had no right to pass through human lips, chanting and wailing with insane fervor. A great tear split the space above the circle. I fired at the leader, but the bullet passed through or around him. Under the hood, an evil, triumphant smile leered out, mocking me. White teeth shined like headlights against the shadows of the hood. He returned his attention to the girl, watching her with intense expectation.

Shooting the cultists had accomplished nothing. The air roiled with a sickening energy that pulsed out of the hovering rip in space.

The ground trembled and hurricane-force winds shook the room. I stood amidst the chaos, powerless to stop the ceremony and save the girl. The statue on the ground projected a bolt of energy through Leslie, up into the rune-covered obelisk, and through the growing portal. The portal expanded, and a tangle of forms boiled forth in a frenzy. Leslie's screams of pain and shock rang through the air. The lead cultist eyed the growing portal, confused by its appearance. He stared at Leslie, seeing the energies of the statue crackle around her without touching. He rushed to check an opened tome on a nearby altar.

I had one bullet left in the barrel. Only one choice remained. I lifted the gun, fired, broke my word, and damned my soul to hell. Time paused as absolute silence fell over the room. No screams, no rumbling, no ambient buzz from the swell of power confined to a tiny room in a dank basement broke that perfect quiet. The bullet struck home, and the world exploded. A thunderous avalanche of sound crashed down. Slumped against the ropes holding her body to the pillar, Leslie hung limp, with a bullet through her skull. Blood covered some of the glyphs on the pillar. The hooded leader cried out in rage and denial.

Great, lashing tendrils, tentacles, claws, and hungry mouths erupted from the rip. The agitated appendages wrapped around and clamped down on the cultists as they screamed for mercy. One claw plucked the body from the obelisk and snatched it up through the tear. As the cultists were dragged into the hovering rent, one of the hooked claws snapped out toward me, grasped my ankle, and pulled me along. A foot made of shadow and charcoal stomped down on the limb. "Not this one," the dark man wearing dark robes intoned. Calm within the raging storm of carnage and suffering, he offered his hand to me. A white smile grew in the middle of his featureless face. I think it was meant to be reassuring, yet a feral, predatory quality warned me that this was a smile few lived to speak about.

My hand took his. The world blinked, and we were standing outside the Silver Twilight Lodge.

"Why?" Words escaped my rattled mind as I stood next to a being well beyond my understanding. A being who was somehow ephemeral and material all at once.

"A favor to a friend. Madam Bina was worried for you."

"Bina?" What did Madam Bina have to do with any of this?

A Rolls Royce hummed around the corner and stalked along the street toward the Lodge. When the headlights fell over the two of us, I turned to witness the man in black evaporate into a dark mist and glide away. When the car stopped, the back door swung open and an ancient, hunched man exited. The metronome tap, thump, thump, announced Sir Mandeville's arrival. He stood there studying the Lodge before addressing me.

"Not the result I expected. You did better than I could have hoped for. Here is a bonus for your impressive work." He reached into his jacket, removed a thick envelope, and tossed it to the ground.

"Better than you hoped?" I growled at him. "I had to kill the girl!"

"Yes! Great stroke of luck that. While I had my own plans for her, better she be eliminated than used against me. This is safer." Mandeville chuckled. "As soon as she disappeared, I tried to kill her, but this Lodge of fools had concealed her from me. Sending detectives, one after the other, bought me time. I never imagined one of you would accomplish the task *for* me."

As he spoke, I searched my pockets for one more bullet. Most had been scattered during the fight and ceremony, but tucked deep down, one had snagged itself into the stitching. I popped the cylinder and slipped the bullet in. I knew the old man would kill me, but if I had to cash in the last morsel of luck I had tonight, he would die, as well. Whipping the gun around, I pulled the trigger. The hammer clicked into silence. Mandeville sneered down on me.

"That didn't work on the fool in the basement. What made you think it would on me? I, who alone have looked upon the Sleeping God. I, who have traveled the celestial pathways to sit at the right hand of Azathoth and whisper my desires into his shattered, insane mind. I could summon a shoggoth here, now, to devour you and delight in your screams." Mandeville shuffled closer. The gem atop his cane shined an array of colors unnamable. "Instead, I leave you here. Nyarlathotep saw fit to spare your life, and so I do as well. Goodbye, Mr. Daniels."

He turned away and entered his car. As it disappeared into the empty streets of Arkham, I struggled to remain on my feet. Stars flickered to life in the night sky. A full, pale moon broke through an invisible curtain to bestow its silvery light upon the world. Somehow, I managed to stagger back to the hotel. In my room, I fell into the bed and passed out. No dreams or nightmares plagued my overwrought mind. Blessed oblivion washed over my battered consciousness.

Coda

The End of a Road

A light knocking at the door broke through the barrier of sleep, protecting me from my recently broken reality. I shuffled across the room, gun in hand, and cracked the door to see who it was. A nervous young man stood holding a slip of paper.

"What?" I barked.

"Um, checkout is in one hour, sir." He extended the paper through the crack. "If you wish to hold the room longer, please come down and speak with the front desk manager."

I took the paper and nodded understanding as I closed the door in the messenger's face. The paper was a handwritten receipt for the money I'd paid at check-in and a notation of how much additional nights would cost. I crumpled the receipt into a ball, arced the wad of paper through the air, and missed the wastebasket by a distance of who cares. After splashing some water on my face, I stuffed my remaining belongings into my duffel and hauled it down to my car. Staring out over the town, I hoped to never set eyes on again. An itch developed in the middle of my muddled brain.

I couldn't shake the feeling I'd missed something important. The events of the case seemed unreal, yet I knew they happened. The fat envelope of cash buried in my bag proved that much. Still, as I replayed the events of the previous night, both mundane and unbelievable, something didn't fit. The rip in the air had surprised the lead cultist. He certainly hadn't expected or intended anything to reach out and pull them all to their end.

And what had Mandeville said? He couldn't locate and assassinate Leslie while she remained under the Lodge's control, even though he considered himself their superior by far. Mandeville didn't strike me as the kind of man who boasted without merit. Something about the entire affair wasn't clicking into place. Every step of the investigation ticked along like a string of dominoes, each one toppling into the next. Somewhere, a missing piece had created an unintended fork that created a new circuit no one had noticed.

After I pressed down the starter paddle, a hunch had me racing along the streets to Miskatonic University. Students were out walking along the marked paths of the campus. Few bothered with the occult library at the corner of College and Garrison. Inside, I found the same kid as before at the front desk. He looked tired and fidgeted when he saw me coming.

"Hey, detective. Any luck?" He tried to smile.

"Rare Books section. Now."

"I would, but..."

"Now," I growled at him, done with the games. Too much had happened.

He froze, eyes flickering one way, then the other, searching for escape.

"Don't, kid." I sighed. "She's not safe. I think I can help." I paused until he met my eyes. "I'll break down that door and find her if I have to. I suggest we do this quietly for her sake and yours."

He nodded and led the way back to the Rare Books room. After locking the door from inside, he motioned for me to follow him into the shadowed stacks. The shelves seemed to go on forever, but soon we took a turn and there, huddled against the wall and wrapped in a blanket sat Leslie Owens, alive and well. Sleep deprived, but alive. She looked up from her notepad to find the sheepish, young librarian leading me straight to her. She struggled to her feet, glaring at him. Rage twisted her tired features as she bristled from what she could only view as betrayal.

"Don't blame him. I knew you were here somewhere and didn't give him much choice." I withdrew the beaten-up picture her parents had given me and offered it to her. "Your mother asked me to find you and get you somewhere safe."

She took the photo and swallowed before asking, "Are they still alive?"

"No. I'm sorry."

"Is he?"

"Mandeville? Yeah, he's alive and the Lodge is dead."

Shock and regret weakened her initial anger. "Oh, God, they killed her?"

"The girl who looked like you? No... They tried to summon something through her, I think. I tried to stop the ceremony, but nothing worked, so I..." My whole body sagged under the weight of it all. "God help me, I shot her, hoping it would stop whatever they were doing. I didn't even know if it would work. I just shot her."

Leslie staggered over to me and wrapped her arms around me. "It's ok. What you killed was just a tulpa. I conjured it and sent it out to be kidnapped once I realized I was in danger."

"A what?"

"A thought form. Like a mystical double. The Lodge wanted to use me to bring forth the Elder Ones and gain control of their technology. Uncle Edward wants something far worse. I've been here, hidden behind all the protections Professor Armitage put in this room, trying to work it out."

"Well, Mandeville thinks you're dead, as well. You should be safe."

"He'll work it out, eventually."

"I know someone who may be able to help us. She likes me, or so I'm told."

Leslie arced her brow, considering my assurance before nodding. She turned to the librarian. "Marcus, I'm going to need to take some of these books with me. I'll get them back as soon as I can."

"You know you can't take them out."

"Kid, this is more important than your library's rules."

"No, I mean, the room won't let them out. The spell Armitage used to protect them from people like the Lodge won't allow it. She knows that."

Leslie began shoving books into an old leather bag that looked far too small for the number she managed to stuff into it. "Don't worry about that. I figured out how to bypass the runes. Armitage provided a failsafe, just in case." She lifted the sack over her shoulder and stood. "Ready when you are." Her clear eyes were steady and without fear.

We left the kid gaping behind us, grumbling and whining about how he was going to get in trouble for the mess and the lost books. At the door, Leslie stepped forward, placed her hand on the knob, and muttered a series of ugly, spidery words. A click triggered in the door, and it swung against the hinges. We strode through the library, wary of any too-curious eyes. In the car, I brought the engine rumbling to life.

"Are you sure you want to help me? Don't know what you've already seen, but..." She hesitated. "There are stories of what happens to people who delve too deeply into this."

"Kid, your mom asked me to keep you safe." I shifted the car into gear. "So, how's about we do that and not go looking for trouble?"

ACKNOWLEDGMENTS

First and foremost, I need to thank Heather Straub. She makes my insane ramblings read as if I were competent. Thanks for that.

Thank you, Stephanie, Yin, and Yang for all the support and faith. Without your support, I would have struggled to find the time, the energy, or the self-belief to keep this going. I want to give a shout-out to all the readers in the Book of Horror Facebook group who supported all my literary efforts and I hope to keep proving myself to you over a hopefully long career.

Thank you to Crystal Lake Entertainment and Joe Mynhardt for supporting my truncated timeline and saving me from having to self-publish. Sorry, and thank you, to everyone who worked so hard to make this a reality. I swear, I'll get the next one done so you won't be overworked because of me.

ABOUT THE AUTHOR

JP Behrens is the author of *Portrait of a Nuclear Family*, *We Don't Talk Anymore and Other Dark Fictions*, and the *Travis Daniels Investigations Series*. A graduate of the Yale Writers' Workshop, he spends his days writing, reading, and practicing Kung Fu. All his other time is spent with family. He looks forward to revisiting sleep one day.

For more from JP Behrens, consider joining his Patreon. A paid membership gives readers a monthly short story, a chapter a month in an ongoing thriller novel, articles, and personal essays. Sometimes, he will send out surprise gifts to his long-term supporters.

THE END?

Not if you want to dive into more of Crystal Lake Publishing's Tales from the Darkest Depths!

Check out our amazing website and online store or download our latest catalog here.
https://geni.us/CLPCatalog

Looking for award-winning Dark Fiction?
Download our latest catalog.
Includes our anthologies, novels, novellas, collections, poetry, non-fiction, and specialty projects.

Where Stories Come Alive!

We always have great new projects and content on the website to dive into, as well as a newsletter, behind the scenes options, social media platforms, our own dark fiction shared-world series and our very own webstore. Our webstore even has categories specifically for KU books, non-fiction, anthologies, and of course more novels and novellas.

Readers…

Thank you for reading *Missing in Miskatonic*. We hope you enjoyed this novella. If you have a moment, please review *Missing in Miskatonic* at the store where you bought it.

Help other readers by telling them why you enjoyed this book. No need to write an in-depth discussion. Even a single sentence will be greatly appreciated. Reviews go a long way to helping a book sell, and is great for an author's career. It'll also help us to continue publishing quality books.

Thank you again for taking the time to journey with Crystal Lake Publishing.

You will find links to all our social media platforms on our Linktree page.
https://linktr.ee/CrystalLakePublishing

Follow us on Amazon:

MISSION STATEMENT

Since its founding in August 2012, Crystal Lake has quickly become one of the world's leading publishers of Dark Fiction and Horror books. In 2023, Crystal Lake officially transitioned into an entertainment company, joining several other divisions, genres, and imprints, including Torrid Waters, Crystal Lake Comics, Crystal Lake Games, Crystal Lake Kids, and many more.

While we strive to present only the highest quality fiction and entertainment, we also endeavour to support authors along their writing journey. We offer our time and experience in non-fiction projects, as well as author mentoring and services, at competitive prices.

With several Bram Stoker Award wins and many other wins and nominations (including the HWA's Specialty Press Award), Crystal Lake Publishing puts integrity, honor, and respect at the forefront of our publishing operations.

We strive for each book and outreach program we spearhead to not only entertain and touch or comment on issues that affect our readers, but also to strengthen and support the Dark Fiction field and its authors.

Not only do we find and publish authors we believe are destined for greatness, but we strive to work with men and women who endeavour to be decent human beings who care more for others than themselves, while still being hard working, driven, and passionate artists and storytellers.

Crystal Lake Publishing is and will always be a beacon of what passion and dedication, combined with overwhelming teamwork and respect, can accomplish. We endeavour to know each and every one of our readers, while building personal relationships with our authors, reviewers, bloggers, podcasters, bookstores, and libraries.

We will be as trustworthy, forthright, and transparent as any business can be, while also keeping most of the headaches away from our authors, since it's our job to solve the problems so they can stay in a creative mind. Which of course also means paying our authors.

We do not just publish books, we present to you worlds within your world, doors within your mind, from talented authors who sacrifice so much for a moment of your time.

There are some amazing small presses out there, and through collaboration and open forums we will continue to support other presses in the goal of helping authors and showing the world what quality small presses are capable of accomplishing. No one wins when a small press goes down, so we will always be there to support hardworking, legitimate presses and their authors. We don't see Crystal Lake as the best press out there, but we will always strive to be the best, strive to be the most interactive and grateful, and even blessed press around. No matter what happens over time, we will also take our mission very seriously while appreciating where we are and enjoying the journey.

What do we offer our authors that they can't do for themselves through self-publishing?

We are big supporters of self-publishing (especially hybrid publishing), if done with care, patience, and planning. However, not every author has the time or inclination to do market research, advertise, and set up book launch strategies. Although a lot of authors are successful in doing it all, strong small presses will always be there for the authors who just want to do what they do best: write.

What we offer is experience, industry knowledge, contacts and trust built up over years. And due to our strong brand and trusting fanbase, every Crystal Lake Publishing book comes with weight of respect. In time our fans begin to trust our judgment and will try a new author purely based on our support of said author.

With each launch we strive to fine-tune our approach, learn from our mistakes, and increase our reach. We continue to assure our authors that we're here for them and that we'll carry the weight of the launch and dealing with third parties while they focus on their strengths—be it writing, interviews, blogs, signings, etc.

We also offer several mentoring packages to authors that include knowledge and skills they can use in both traditional and self-publishing endeavours.

We look forward to launching many new careers.

This is what we believe in. What we stand for. This will be our legacy.

Welcome to Crystal Lake Publishing—Where Stories Come Alive!

www.ingramcontent.com/pod-product-compliance
Lightning Source LLC
LaVergne TN
LVHW012121070526
838202LV00056B/5821